Contents

Chapter One

The heart of Merryvale Shopping Mall pulsed with chaotic festivity. Twinkling lights flickered wildly, wreaths hung aimlessly, and the animatronic penguins, which had seen better days, buzzed and jerked in a disconcerting dance that could only be described as something straight out of a nightmare. The air was filled with the faint jingling of bells and the relentless hum of Christmas music that had long since overstayed its welcome. Towering above it all, the massive Christmas tree stood as a beacon of joy for anyone whose soul was yet to be destroyed by the season's relentless mayhem. Beneath its branches sat Santa - a man so utterly absorbed in his role that he refused to respond to any other name.

In his eyes, he wasn't playing Santa. He *was Santa*, and Santa lived for this.

This wasn't just a seasonal gig; it was his calling. Every December, he returned to his throne at Merryvale, surrounded by fake snow and his trusty elves. It was the time of year he longed for. Like how Michael Myers longed for Halloween, no other season mattered.

Children eagerly queued to meet him, tugging at their parents' sleeves and bouncing excitedly. The first child of the day, a girl no older than five in a festive reindeer sweater, stood beside Santa, clutching a well-loved stuffed bear as if it were her most prized possession.

Santa smiled behind his thick, genuine white beard.

"I'm Emily! I want a Danny Demon action figure with a moving chainsaw add-on, a rotating head, and extra blood vomit cartridges!" she exclaimed, her eyes sparkling with excitement.

Santa chuckled, his belly wobbling like a bowl full of jelly. "Well... I'm not sure that's *appropriate*," he said softly, raising an eyebrow at the ambitious request.

When he noticed the offended looks from her parents, he quickly changed course. "But who am I to judge? Emily, Santa will see what he can do."

"Thank you, Santa!" she squealed.

"Now, how about a picture with Santa, once my elf is ready?" he asked, beaming.

Beside him stood Lily, the elf, a petite young woman with sparkling eyes and a warm, friendly smile. Her chestnut hair was pulled into playful pigtails, giving her that "girl next door" charm. Her elf costume clung to her figure just enough to be festive and cute, complete with striped tights and floppy green shoes.

To Santa's growing frustration, Lily was distracted. Liz Lang, Merryvale's Marketing Manager, had pulled the girl aside to film a silly dance for their social media.

Liz, the self-proclaimed social media guru, had gone viral years ago with one of her dances, and she'd been chasing those numbers ever since - never managing to hit the million mark. Not even close.

She had tried, numerous times, to get Santa to dance for her, but he always refused. He hated the modern world. He took it personally that kids were no longer allowed to sit on his lap. He also hated that he couldn't take a swig of brandy on especially tough days. Times had changed, and while he was willing to adapt to most things, parading around like a dancing monkey for 'likes' was not one of them.

When Lily finally finished her performance, Santa cleared his throat loudly to grab her attention.

"*Sorry*," she called out, rushing back.

Liz glanced at Santa, her phone in hand, and asked, "You sure you won't do one little video?"

"I'm *sure*."

"Fine," she sulked, turning away in defeat.

Lily quickly snapped a photo, the flash illuminating the joyful scene as Emily's eyes sparkled with delight.

"Merry Christmas, Emily!" Santa and Lily chirped in unison, their voices full of cheer.

"*Merry Christmas*!" Emily shouted back, her joy infectious as she skipped off to her parents. The thrill of the moment was palpable in every excited bounce of her little feet.

Moments like these made it all worthwhile.

Santa poured his heart and soul into this role. He spent the entire year preparing for it - perfecting his laugh and memorising toy trends. One year, he even endured a marathon of watching Frozen seven times in a row just so that he would understand the references. By the end of that particular grind, he didn't want to build a snowman; he wanted to obliterate one with a fucking flamethrower.

But it was worth it. *All of it.* Because for a few moments, every child felt the magic of Christmas. It wasn't just about the toys - it was about the joy. Pure, unfiltered joy.

The next child in line was a small boy, maybe four years old, with wide, curious eyes peeking out from beneath an oversized woollen hat stitched with a truck. He wore a matching truck-themed coat, truck-themed gloves, truck-themed trainers - truck *everything*!

His parents stood behind him, their expressions tense as they encouraged him forward.

The boy, however, wasn't having it. He stopped about two feet from Santa, his little face scrunched up in determination.

"Well, hello there!" Santa said with a booming laugh. "And what's your name, young man?"

The boy stayed silent, staring up at Santa with a mix of awe and suspicion. After a moment of awkward silence, the boy crossed his arms.

"Are you *really* Santa?" he finally asked, his voice small but firm.

Santa smiled under his beard, amused by the boy's seriousness. "*Of course*! Who else would I be? I've come all the way from the North Pole!"

The boy squinted, clearly unconvinced. "*Prove it*."

Santa leaned forward, his eyes twinkling.

"Well, let's see..."

Santa tapped his nose thoughtfully. "How about *this*? Last year, I brought you a toy truck, right?"

The boy's mouth fell open. To him, it was nothing short of a miracle.

"*Whoa*," the boy whispered, his suspicion replaced by awe.

"Now," Santa said with a smile, "do you believe?"

The boy hesitated for a moment, then gave a serious nod. "*Yes.*'

Santa let out a hearty laugh. "Good lad! So, how about a picture to remember this moment?"

The elf snapped the photo, and the boy marched back to his parents with newfound excitement.

Next in line was a girl around twelve years old. She marched up to Santa with a purposeful stride, her expression deadly serious.

"Ho, ho, h—" Santa began, but she cut him off with a wave of her hand.

"Let's skip the pleasantries," she said, her voice sharp, her gaze unwavering.

"...Alright," Santa replied, sitting up a little straighter. "What's on your mind?"

"My neighbour ran over my dog," she said bluntly, her voice trembling as tears welled in her eyes.

Santa's heart clenched. "Oh, I'm so sorry to hear that," he said gently. "Would you like me to bring you a new dog?"

"No," she snapped, her expression hardening. "I want a gun so I can shoot the bastard who did it."

The air seemed to freeze. Santa's jovial demeanour faltered, his mouth falling open in shock. "I, uh... I don't think I ca--"

Before he could finish, the girl's father stepped in, cutting off the moment. He was tall, sharply dressed in an expensive suit, his eyes cold and calculating.

"*Here*," the man said quietly, pulling a small gift box from his pocket and thrusting it into Santa's hands. "Give her this. It's a Tiffany necklace. I don't want her taking your cheap, tacky shopping mall shit into my home."

Santa stared at the box, utterly stunned, before croaking out a reluctant, "*Okay*."

The father stepped aside, and Santa handed the box to the girl, who snatched it without so much as a glance at him. She tore it open on the spot, her face falling into an incredulous scowl as she inspected the contents.

"Where are the fucking diamonds?" she demanded, her voice rising in fury.

Her father crossed his arms, glaring at Santa as though this were somehow his fault. "You'd better sort your shit out before Christmas Day," he said icily. "*Unbelievable*."

With that, the pair turned and stormed off, their indignation trailing behind them like a bad smell.

Santa exchanged a glance with Lily. For a moment, they both held their composure - but then, the absurdity of it all overwhelmed them. They burst into laughter, the sound echoing through the makeshift North Pole.

This was what it was all about - the unpredictability of it all. You never knew what these kids, and sometimes the *parents*, were going to say.

Throughout the morning, the requests ranged from the bizarre to the downright impossible. One child earnestly asked for a giant trampoline to reach the moon, eyes wide with wonder at the possibility. Another insisted on having "two turtle doves," but not the birds from the classic song. No, he wanted twisted, freakish hybrids - half turtle, half dove - like something dreamt up by Dr. Frankenstein himself.

As the queue inched forward, something dark flickered in the corner of Santa's eye.

At the back of the line, a pack of teenagers lingered, their posture loose and predatory, smirks plastered on their faces. They weren't here for Christmas cheer. Their phones were already out- cameras rolling, capturing everything before it even began. Santa's well-practised smile remained in place, but an icy knot twisted in his gut.

Something was wrong.

Each child that passed felt like a blur, and Santa's "ho, ho, ho" became hollow. The dread clung to him, thickening with every breath. When the teens finally reached the front of the line, his heart lurched.

The leader stepped forward - a lanky boy with greasy hair, his swagger exaggerated, eyes gleaming with mockery. He plopped onto Santa's lap with a real smugness about him. His friends closed in around them, phones raised like knives, filming the scene with an anticipation that made Santa's skin crawl.

"Oi, Santa," the boy sneered, voice dripping with malice. "How about giving me something decent this year? All I got last Christmas was Steve's mum."

He jerked a thumb toward one of his friends, who teased back, "Yeah, *you wish* you could stuff her stocking."

Santa's smile twitched, the weight of the situation settling in his bones. "Now, boys, let's keep it *festive*," he said, but his usual hearty tone wavered, betraying the crack in his composure. "How about a picture, and you can move along?"

The boy's grin widened. He leaned in close, his breath sour with cheap energy drinks and cigarettes. "Nah, for real this time, Santa. What I *really* want is to fuck your little elf over there. Maybe deliver her wearing nothing but a cute pink bow."

He flicked his gaze to Lily, and Santa's blood ran cold.

The laughter that erupted from the group was cruel, and jagged, cutting through the holiday warmth with violent force.

Families nearby were already retreating, pulling their children away from the scene, whispering anxiously.

Santa's heart pounded in his chest, a thrumming pulse of helplessness and fury.

"That's *enough*!" he barked, his voice strained, trying desperately to cling to some semblance of control. "Don't be so *vulgar*!"

The boy only laughed harder, sensing weakness. "What's up, Santa? You don't like to share your toys?"

Santa's gaze darted to Lily. She stood frozen a few feet away, her face drained of all colour. Her hands trembled as she clutched the hem of her festive costume, the playful elf façade crumbling. Fear flickered in her wide eyes - fear that Santa could feel down to his core.

The boy rose from Santa's lap, swaggering toward her with the confidence of someone who knew no one would stop him. "Hey, *sweetheart*", he drawled, licking his lips. "Let me have a play with your baubles." With that, he reached out for her breasts.

Lily's breath hitched, and she backed into the decorative display behind her.

"*Stop it*," she whispered, voice shaky but filled with defiance. "Seriously, *fuck off*!"

The boy's grin twisted into something darker. "Oh, I like it when they fight back," he taunted, his hand reaching out to tug at one of her pigtails. "Bet you're *right up there* on that naughty list."

The other boys surged closer, a mass of sneering faces and outstretched hands, their cameras still rolling.

Another one grabbed Lily's arm, yanking her toward him. "Come on, babe. Have a picture with us and then we'll leave you alone."

Santa's heart hammered in his chest, his vision blurring with rage. The cheerful world of Christmas lights and children's laughter seemed to fade, swallowed by the sickening reality unfolding in front of him. "Get your *hands off her*!" Santa roared, his voice booming, shaking the very air around them.

He stood so suddenly that the chair beneath him rattled, threatening to topple over.

But the boys didn't even flinch. They turned to him, laughing, the sneers cutting deep. "Santa, that's *not* very jolly of you," the leader mocked, stepping even closer to Lily, his gaze leering at her with vile intent. "Don't worry about her. She *loves it*."

Fury coiled within Santa like a beast ready to strike. His hands trembled as he lunged forward, seizing the boy's arm in a crushing grip. He yanked him back with a force that sent the boy stumbling, his cocky expression shattering as he hit the ground.

"*Piss off*!" Santa growled, his voice thick with fury. "All of you! *Now*!"

For a brief, electric moment, the boy's laughter died, replaced by a look of shock. But it didn't last. The leader scrambled to his feet, his face twisted with rage and embarrassment. "You're fucked,

Santa," he spat, backing away, his friends close behind. "You're *so* done."

One of them muttered under his breath, loud enough for Santa to hear. "This shit's going *viral*."

They slunk off into the crowd, their laughter still trailing behind them like the aftermath of a storm. But now, there was something darker to it - something that promised more trouble.

Santa stood there, his chest heaving, his hands still trembling from the surge of adrenaline. The festive cheer around him felt distant, muffled, as if the entire mall had turned to ash. Slowly, he turned to Lily.

She was pale, her body trembling as she hugged herself tightly, eyes wide with terror. He had failed her. Failed to protect her. Failed to keep this twisted moment from shattering the innocence of the holiday season.

For the first time in his long career as Santa Claus, the joy of Christmas felt like it was slipping through his fingers. As he stood there, watching the fear in Lily's eyes, Santa realised the true horror of the moment - this was only the beginning.

Chapter Two

Santa's home stood at the edge of town, sagging under the weight of neglect. The wood of the cabin's walls was warped and weather-beaten, with patches of rot creeping up from the ground. The roof, missing a few shingles, slumped as though tired of bearing the load of snow that piled on it every winter. The windows, caked in grime, were cracked in places, their edges lined with cheap, peeling plastic as a feeble attempt to keep out the biting cold.

But despite the decay, the house still clung desperately to a twisted sense of festivity. Every inch of the rundown property was adorned with Christmas decorations. Strings of lights, many flickering or completely burnt out, were draped haphazardly over the gutters. Faded plastic reindeer, missing parts of their antlers and chipped beyond recognition, stood lopsided in the front yard. An ancient inflatable Santa slouched near the front door, perpetually half-deflated, giving it a sunken, almost defeated look. It was clear that whatever little money Santa had went into these decorations, as though they were the only things holding his life together.

Inside was no better. The floors creaked underfoot, the boards splintering and uneven. The walls were bare except for a few old Christmas-themed paintings and tattered stockings that hadn't been taken down in years. The living room was dominated by a massive Christmas tree, but even that looked exhausted — its branches drooping, the ornaments chipped and mismatched, some held together by fraying strings.

Santa, hunched over at his kitchen table, stared at his phone with hollow eyes.

A ping echoed in the silence, followed by another.

Santa frowned, glancing at his phone. His heart sank as he saw the first message from an unknown number.

"You're famous, Santa!"

Another ping.

"Saw the video! Man, you're fucked up!"

He blinked, confusion slowly giving way to dread. His hand shook as he opened yet another message. A link. Hesitantly, he clicked it.

The video opened mid-chaos. There was no footage of the vulgar comments, no sound of the boy's sneers or the crude jokes hurled at Lily. It started right at the moment of Santa's outburst, skipping everything that had led to it.

The clip showed Santa, red-faced and towering, his hands clenched into fists as he bellowed, his voice echoing in the cavernous mall. The camera zoomed in on his furious expression, capturing the moment he grabbed the boy by the arm. The sound of him hitting the floor was amplified, his sprawled form shown in slow motion, making Santa's movements look monstrous. The festive lights twinkled mockingly in the background as the shoppers around them recoiled, wide-eyed, stepping back in fear.

In the footage, the mall was silent, as though even the air had been sucked out of the room. No laughter from the boys, no jeering taunts — just a disorienting hush as Santa stood, his chest heaving, his eyes blazing with fury. The camera held on to that image for a few seconds too long, making him look almost unhinged, as if he were barely keeping himself from attacking again.

Then came the voiceover, a YouTuber's dramatic narration: "This is Merryvale Mall's Santa Claus... and apparently, he's had *enough*." Clips from different angles showed the same moment — Santa's hands gripping the boy, his enraged shout — replayed over and over, each time with Santa looking more and more like a man on the verge of violence. "I don't know what happened here, but this guy... he *snapped*. And these poor kids... they must have been *terrified*."

Not a single word about the teens' behaviour. Nothing about the harassment, the foul jokes, the fear in Lily's eyes. Only Santa, in the middle of his furious outburst, made to look like a lunatic who had turned on the children he was supposed to bring joy to.

Santa's stomach dropped as he watched the video loop again, feeling the noose of public opinion tighten around his neck. They had erased the truth. The kids were painted as innocent bystanders, and he was the monster who had ruined Christmas.

He quickly closed the video, but his phone wouldn't stop buzzing.

Ping. Another message. Another link.

He clicked it, almost on autopilot, dread sinking into his stomach.

A bubbly young woman appeared on screen, wearing glittery reindeer antlers. Behind her, an overly decorated Christmas tree twinkled with oversized ornaments and garish tinsel. "Okay, everyone, we all love Santa, right?" she asked her mass following, her glittery reindeer antlers bouncing with each word. "Well, maybe not *this one*. This psychopath totally snapped at some poor, terrified teenagers. And get this - according to the young victims, they were just trying to hand him a letter for their dead cousin who never got to deliver it himself!" She paused dramatically, and a 'sad' emoji popped onto the screen, followed by the sound of a sombre bell.

Santa's eyes bulged as he stared at the screen. "*What?! That's a lie!*" he roared.

His hands trembled, fumbling to close the video.

Ping. Another link.

He couldn't stop himself. Maybe the next video would show someone with an ounce of common sense - someone stating that there could be more to this story.

No. *Of course not.*

It was a video of a grinning country singer in a cowboy hat, guitar in hand, strumming away.

A familiar tune began, but the lyrics had been twisted;

"You better watch out,
You better not cry,
You better not laugh,
I'm telling you why:
Santa Claus has lost his goddamn mind!"

Santa winced, his fingers digging into the phone as the singer continued:

"He's not full of joy,
He's not full of cheer,
He's yelling at kids,
After too many beers,
Santa Claus has lost his goddamn mi—"

Santa closed the video, his heart sinking deeper into his chest. "Oh no, ho, ho," he groaned, the pitiful sound echoing against the chipped walls of his decrepit home. The lies were everywhere. Everyone was turning against him, and no one - absolutely *no one* - seemed to care about the truth. The reality of the situation simply wasn't as interesting as the narrative being spun around him.

His hands shook, his breath coming in shallow gasps as the weight of the online world pressed down on his chest. Christmas had always been his life, but now it felt like it was slipping away from him, taking his grip on reality along with it.

Most of the videos discussing the incident featured thumbnails of him looking furious, but one stood out and made his blood run cold. It was the ringleader, the boy who had humiliated him in front of everyone.

Reluctantly, Santa clicked on the video. The boy appeared on screen, sitting in his bedroom, his greasy hair combed neatly for once, his voice laced with false innocence.

"Hey, guys," he began, eyes wide and shimmering with fake tears. "I just... I need to talk about what happened today." He sniffed, wiping his nose for dramatic effect. "It was supposed to be a special day, you know? Fulfilling a final wish." The boy paused, swallowing hard. "I didn't expect to be attacked by... Santa. I don't know what I did to make him so mad. I... I was scared. I really thought he was going to kill me. It may take a while for the emotional scars to start healing. If you guys can donate to my GoFundMe page, I'll be able to afford some counselling to help speed up the process."

His voice cracked as he wiped at his eyes again, his followers flooding the comments with messages of sympathy. "And don't be too cheap, guys. I need a new PlayStation too."

Santa's heart pounded in his chest, despair thickening the air around him. He couldn't breathe. Couldn't think. They were painting him as a monster, turning him into a joke - a villain. He had dedicated his life to keeping Christmas alive, to spreading joy, and this was how they repaid him? By ruining his life and turning him into a meme?

Then came the final blow: an email.

It was from the shopping mall's owner, that arrogant young man who had reluctantly kept him hired only because his dying father had convinced him to do so.

"Come to my office first thing tomorrow. No need to bring the costume."

Santa's face twisted with anger. *Costume*? He wasn't wearing a *costume*. This was who he was. This wasn't just a job; it wasn't an act. He *was* Santa Claus.

His hand clenched around his phone, knuckles turning white as he slammed it down on the table.

The festive decorations blinked weakly in the background, their glow mocking him.

For the first time, the magic of Christmas felt like a burden. The joy he had spent his life trying to spread now tasted bitter, poisoned by mockery and hatred.

He marched toward the bedroom, slowly opening the door. "Mrs. Claus? You awake?"

"What's wrong, Santa?" came the gentle reply.

Santa broke down into tears. "It's over, Mrs. Claus. It's all over."

Chapter Three

Santa sat heavily in a leather chair, his red suit worn and faded. It had never appeared that way until now. It was as if the Christmas magic was truly gone.

The jingle bells on his hat jingled softly, mocking the silence in the room. His hands were clasped tightly together in his lap. His eyes fixed on the polished surface of the desk before him, but his mind was elsewhere - lost in memories of laughter, eager children, and Christmas joy.

The room was filled with a suffocating tension that pressed down on Santa's chest as every second ticked by. He had faced the hustle of Christmas Eve, weathered endless demands for gifts, handled crying babies and overexcited toddlers. He had always found joy in it, always found purpose. But now, sitting in front of these three cold, scrutinising faces, Santa felt something he hadn't in centuries: heartache.

Across from him sat Kieran Poole, the mall's owner, a young man with more inherited wealth than wisdom. Kieran lounged in his plush leather chair, spinning a gold pen between his fingers as if he were some business pro, rather than a guy who'd stumbled into his father's empire by sheer luck. His shirt was half unbuttoned, his hair slicked back to an almost cartoonish shine, and a pair of sunglasses rested on his head for no apparent reason.

Santa had adored Kieran's father - a man full of kindness, who always made time to chat and understood the true spirit of Christmas. How someone so generous and gentle had raised someone as self-serving and callous as Kieran was beyond Santa's comprehension.

"Listen, Claus," Kieran began, his voice oozing apathy, "if it's any consolation, this would've been your last year either way. We're going with VR next season."

Santa's heart tightened. *"VR?"*

Kieran stifled a chuckle. "Virtual Reality. We'll save a fortune. Instead of bringing the North Pole here, we'll send the kids there... digitally... for a much greater price. They don't have to visit the North Pole, of course. Maybe they'll visit Santa on... the moon! Or perhaps during the days of the dinosaurs." He leaned back even further, a smug grin spreading across his face. "The possibilities are *endless.*"

Santa felt the weight of those words. Virtual reality? How could a screen replace the warmth of a shared moment, the joy of a child's laughter as they tugged on his beard to see if it was real? How could they replace the twinkle in his eye, the promise of magic that had been passed down through generations?

"But that's not what Christmas is," Santa said quietly, his voice tinged with sorrow.

Kieran waved him off with a dismissive hand. "Nostalgia's not paying the bills, Claus. It's time to move on. You're done. And after yesterday's fiasco? You should be thankful we're not pressing charges."

Santa opened his mouth to defend himself, but before he could, Liz Lang jumped in, her jittery energy filling the room like static. "We're in full-blown crisis mode because of *you*, Santa!" she said frantically, flailing her arms. "I mean, you broke the internet - and not in a good way! You're *everywhere*! I overheard a mother this morning warning her son that if he didn't stop being a naughty little shit, the Merryvale Santa would come and get him. That little brat shut the fuck up *immediately*."

Santa's chest tightened further. "I didn't mean t--"

Liz cut him off, her voice shrill. "Doesn't matter! Society has already voted. You're guilty in the court of public opinion. They have... cancelled you. And if we were to allow you to continue working here... they'll cancel *us too*."

The words stung. Santa had been many things over the centuries - bringer of joy, keeper of dreams - but never the villain.

Then Lord Steeler, seated beside Liz, cleared his throat with an air of theatrical importance, desperate for the spotlight. "If I may interject," he began, his voice oozing smugness. His cheap Santa suit hung awkwardly on his wiry frame, as if even the fabric wanted to distance itself from him. "I just want to assure you, the role of Father Christmas is in very safe hands. My extensive background in theatre and cinema makes me uniquely qualified for this position."

Liz, practically preening beside him, added with a smirk, "We only hired him a few hours ago, and he's already filmed five dances for our socials."

She folded her arms, as if daring Santa to argue, the glow of self-satisfaction radiating off her like a neon sign.

Santa stared at the man who dared to claim his throne, hardly believing what he was hearing. Lord Steeler - whose most notable recent "performance" involved being the rear end of the horse in Werrington Village Hall's ill-fated adaptation of Black Beauty - thought he could simply step into the boots of Father Christmas?

It was laughable. Santa wasn't a role you played; it wasn't a costume you donned or a script you memorised. Being Santa was a way of being. It was something you carried in your heart, something you lived and breathed every day. It was about believing in magic, embodying selfless generosity, and giving - not for applause or recognition, but because it was simply the right thing to do.

This man, this "actor", *didn't even have a real beard.* Santa prided himself on his beard - full, white, and authentic, a symbol of his dedication. How could this pretender even begin to understand what it truly meant to be Santa?

Before Santa could voice his frustration, the door creaked open, and in walked Conner, the mall's overeager security guard. Or, more accurately, a wannabe cop. Conner strutted in with a swagger that screamed of someone desperate for authority, but it was impossible to take him seriously. His badge, handcuffs, and hat were clearly from a toy set - a fact Santa knew all too well. After all, he'd handed out hundreds of identical plastic accessories over the years to kids who also dreamed of playing a police officer.

"It's time for you to *leave*, Claus," Conner said, his voice attempting authority but landing somewhere between flat and bored.

Santa's chest tightened. He felt the weight of three decades of service crashing down on him. Thirty years of listening to children's dreams, watching families grow, and carrying the spirit of Christmas in his heart. And now? He was being discarded like a broken ornament.

"You're making a mistake," Santa said, his voice steady but tinged with sorrow. "I've been this mall's Santa for more than thirty years. I've seen children grow up, who now bring *their own* kids to visit me. I am Merryvale's Santa."

Kieran, leaning against the wall with a cigarette twitching between his fingers, glanced at his watch and shrugged. "Yeah, well… everything comes to an end. Now hurry up, because this firing malarkey is stressing me out, and I need a smoke."

Santa rose from his chair slowly, the creak of his knees echoing in the silent room. The weight of years - of memories, joy, and the love he'd poured into this role - settled into his bones like lead. Straightening his red coat, he turned to face them one last time. Liz, Lord Steeler, Kieran, and Conner - they all stood there, indifferent, unable or unwilling to see the heart of the man before them.

"Out of curiosity," Santa asked softly, his hand on the door handle, "does anyone actually want to hear the *truth* about what happened?"

The room remained silent. Not a single word, not even a glance.

"And you're all *absolutely certain* that firing me is the right thing to do?" he pressed.

They nodded in unison, the weight of their collective coldness crushing him.

Conner moved in, grabbing Santa's arm with unnecessary force. The once-proud embodiment of Christmas found himself dragged through the shopping mall like some kind of freakish sideshow attraction. People stopped to stare, their whispers swirling around him like icy winds.

By the time they reached the exit, Conner shoved Santa out the doors with little ceremony, the harsh chill of the outdoors biting at him. The humiliation wasn't over, though. As Santa stumbled, he collided head-on with a suited man carrying a steaming cup of coffee - the same pompous father who had handed over the Tiffany necklace the day before.

The collision sent the coffee flying, splattering across the man's expensive suit. He let out an enraged growl, staring at the stain as though it had personally insulted him. "You absolute *dickhead*! This suit costs more than you make in a year!" he roared.

Santa said nothing, too drained to respond.

The man stormed off, muttering curses under his breath, leaving Santa to stare down at his own stained red outfit.

It was as if the collision had stripped away the last remnants of magic his own festive suit once held. It hung heavy and lifeless, a symbol of what he'd lost.

Standing alone in the cold, Santa's sorrow hardened into something darker. His fists clenched at his sides as he glared back at the mall, its glowing lights mocking him.

"You'll pay," he muttered, his voice low and venomous. His gaze burned with the promise of retribution. "You'll *all* pay."

Chapter Four

Santa sat hunched over in his creaky armchair, the springs groaning beneath his weight as the wind outside howled through the cracks in the windows. Across from him, in an old, worn rocking chair, sat Mrs. Claus - or what was left of her.

Her skin hung in ragged strips, grey and green with decay, patches missing to reveal the bone beneath. Her once plump face had sunken, hollowed. Her lips were shrivelled and cracked, the teeth beneath sharp in the dim light. And yet, Santa gazed at her with adoration, his eyes sparkling with twisted affection.

She had been dead for quite a while, but not in Santa's mind. To him, she was full of life - perfect as ever.

"I can't believe it," he muttered, rubbing his hands together as he stared lovingly into his wife's empty eye sockets. His voice cracked with anger. "After all these years. They flung me out like an unwanted toy. Can you believe it?"

Mrs. Claus's head moved, creaking on its thin, brittle neck. *"Fired? You?"* Her voice was raspy, dry, like wind scraping across a frozen grave. "Oh, my love… how awful. Sounds like they've been very… *naughty*."

He looked up, his face contorting with frustration. "They're the worst of the worst, those people. Suits. Big office types. Only caring about the bottom line. No wonder Christmas magic is dying."

Mrs. Claus grinned, her skeletal smile stretching too far, the skin around her lips cracking as she leaned forward. "Well, my dear… you can't let that stand, can you?"

His face softened. "No. I can't. *I won't.*"

Santa's mind began to wonder. He was often haunted by the day Mrs. Claus died. A truly unfortunate night.

He could still remember it like it was yesterday. The way she had stormed into their home, her face flushed with anger, her voice trembling with frustration. She had stood in front of him, hands on her hips, daring to say what no one had ever dared say to him before.

"*This is ridiculous*! *I can't do this anymore, Charles*!" she had shouted, her voice quivering.

"My name is *Santa*!"

"*No*! No it's *not*! And it's not even Christmas. You're pretending to be Santa... in *July*! It's boiling out. You're obsessed. You've lost yourself in this… this *madness*. I want a divorce. I'm leaving you!"

The word had hit him like a sledgehammer to the chest. Divorce. She wanted to leave. To abandon him.

His breath had quickened, but he stayed calm, eerily so. "You can't leave me," he had said quietly, his eyes narrowing. "I love you... Mrs. Claus."

"I'm not Mrs. Clause! Not *anymore*!"

"Sweetie. Baby. *I love you.*"

"Well... I... I don't love you anymore," she confessed, tears brimming in her eyes. "I'm sorry, Charles. I fell out of love with you a long time ago."

That was when something inside him broke. He'd reached for the nearest thing - a snow globe sitting on the mantle, delicate and festive - and brought it crashing down on her skull. She had stumbled back, her hands reaching up to her head, eyes wide with disbelief.

"Charles... what...?" Her voice had trailed off, gurgling as blood trickled down her forehead.

But he didn't stop. The snow globe came down again and again, the glass shattering, mixing with the blood pooling at her feet. She had collapsed, limp and silent, but still, he hadn't stopped. He couldn't stop.

When the rage had finally burned itself out, he stood there, panting, looking down at what was left of her. She was still Mrs. Claus. She'd always be Mrs. Claus. She still loved him. And now, she could *never* leave him.

Back in the present, Santa chuckled softly to himself, the sound hollow in the dark, cold room. He looked over at her once more, her decayed face still twisted in that grotesque grin.

"Look at us," he said softly, his voice thick with adoration. "I may have lost my job, but at least I'll always have you."

Mrs. Claus's head wobbled again, that strange, hollow rasp escaping her lips. "Of course, my love. But those bastards still need to be *punished*."

Santa smiled, his eyes gleaming. He stood, his heavy boots thudding against the floor as he paced, the bells on his belt jingling faintly. "They do, don't they." He pulled a sharpened candy cane from his coat pocket, twisting it in his hands, the tip gleaming ominously. "They'll get what they deserve. Every single one of them."

Mrs. Claus's head tilted slightly, her grin widening further as her bones creaked. "Yes... make them pay, Santa. Make them pay *dearly*."

Santa leaned down, pressing a soft kiss to her cold, lifeless forehead, his gloved hand brushing her cheek as though she were still warm, still his beautiful wife. "For you, my love. Always for you."

Chapter Five

Kieran leaned against the railing of Merryvale Shopping Mall's upper balcony, his eyes sweeping across the chaos below. Where most might see frantic last-minute shoppers darting from store to store, arms overflowing with bags, or children eagerly tugging their parents towards the candy kiosks, Kieran saw only one thing - dollar signs. Every hand pulling out a credit card rang in his mind like the cha-ching of a cash register. His lips curled into a smug smirk. This wasn't just a holiday rush; it was a goldmine, and he was right on top of it.

Beside the business owner stood Liz, clutching her tablet, her fingers flying across the screen as she scrolled through an endless list of schedules, social media updates, and crisis management notes. The viral Santa attack video still lingered over them like a dark cloud. She was trying to focus on her plans to fix their reputation, but the noise from the floor below kept cutting through her concentration. Laughter, shouts, and the ever-present whiny voices of impatient children blended, a cacophony of holiday stress.

"You're *not real*!" one kid wailed loudly from the Christmas village below, the sharp sound making Liz wince. "You don't look like Santa!"

From their vantage point, they could just make out the figure of Lord Steeler, sitting stiffly on the velvet throne. He looked almost comically pompous, draped in a too-large Santa suit that hung awkwardly on his thin frame, the fake white beard doing little to hide his permanent scowl. The kid in front of him looked up, wide-eyed and sceptical, tugging on his mom's sleeve.

"He doesn't even sound like Santa!" the child said to her, his voice piercing through the noise of the mall.

Steeler leaned towards the boy, his fake beard shifting as he spoke in a typical aristocratic tone. His theatrical voice booming out, echoing off the tile floors, dripping with condescension. "Well, I am *so sorry* that Santa has learned to pronounce his words *correctly*," he retorted, dragging out the words as though lecturing a room of dim-witted students. "Now, what do you want for Christmas? And speak clearly, please."

A young weary elf - wearing a wrinkled, ill-fitting costume - hurried the family out of the area before Lord Steeler could do any more damage. The kid's mother cast a sideways glance at Steeler, muttering under her breath as she led her son away.

Kieran let out a heavy sigh, rubbing his temples. "I am so *done* with Santas," he muttered, his voice dripping with exasperation. "Thank God tomorrow's Christmas Eve. After that, we can wash our hands of this Santa nonsense for good. Creepy bastards, *the lot of them*."

Liz barely glanced up from her tablet. "Speaking of Christmas Eve," she said briskly, her fingers dancing across the screen, "Lee Lauren is scheduled to arrive ten minutes before his DJ set tomorrow. It's going to be tight, but if we can keep the mall floor clear and manage the crowds, it should go smoothly."

Kieran shot her a sharp look, the irritation radiating off him. "*Ten minutes? Are you serious?* We're paying him a *bloody fortune*, Liz. He should be here whenever we damn well tell him to be."

Liz didn't flinch at his tone; she was used to his tantrums by now. "Kieran, the only reason we still have customers in this mall right now is because of Lee Lauren. That Santa fiasco has gone viral everywhere, and it's not doing us any favours. Lee Lauren is the only thing keeping this sinking ship afloat. Trust me, if you think today's busy, just wait until tomorrow. We *need* him... regardless of how little time he's giving us."

Kieran grumbled under his breath, running a hand through his slicked-back hair. "And he still insists on those foam cannons during his set?"

"He does," Liz confirmed without looking up.

"That just sounds like an accident waiting to happen."

"It's no different from people walking into the mall soaked from the rain," Liz countered, her tone clipped but reasonable.

"...*Fine*," Kieran relented with a gruff exhale, throwing his hands in the air.

Liz returned to her tablet, the rapid tapping of her fingers filling the silence. After a moment, she hesitated, a flicker of doubt crossing her face. Pausing, she glanced up at Kieran again. "You're sure Conner's the right person to handle things tomorrow? He can be a little... overzealous. And after what happened with the Santa incident, we really can't afford *another* PR disaster."

Kieran waved her concern away with a dismissive hand. "He'll be *fine*. I'll have a word with him."

Liz raised an eyebrow but decided against pressing further. Her attention snapped back to her screen as Kieran muttered something about needing a cigarette, leaving her alone with her thoughts and the uneasy feeling settling in her chest.

In the Merryvale Mall's conference room, a ragtag group of security-for-hire recruits lounged around, their mismatched uniforms and casual postures making it clear this wasn't exactly an elite squad. They sipped on energy drinks and nibbled on cheap biscuits, chatting idly as they waited for training to begin - training that was already twenty minutes behind schedule.

Conner, the self-appointed leader, stood off to the side, propping one foot on a chair as though striking a heroic pose. His booming voice dominated the room, aimed at a wide-eyed recruit who hung onto every word like Conner was some legendary lawman instead of a glorified mall cop.

"I could've been in the police force, you know," Conner bragged, puffing out his chest like a rooster. His tone was steeped in unwarranted confidence, the kind of swagger that only came from rehearsing one's lies too many times. "But when I went for the interview, they said I was *too good*. Said I'd be snatched up by the FBI in no time, and they didn't want to waste their resources on someone destined for greater things."

The recruit's eyes widened, practically glowing with admiration. "That's incredible! Did you ever think about joining the FBI?"

For a fleeting moment, panic flickered across Conner's face. He clearly hadn't anticipated follow-up questions. But in true Conner fashion, he recovered with a cocky grin. "Nah," he said, leaning closer to his audience. "You seen the women that come through this mall? They can't resist a guy in uniform. For lunch, if I ain't eating fried chicken from the food court, I'm eating pussy. Why would I want to give that up?" He gestured to the toy badge and oversized handcuffs hanging from his belt like they were golden artefacts of authority.

The recruit glanced at the cheap plastic accessories and nodded earnestly. "Yeah... that makes sense."

Satisfied, Conner turned back to the rest of the room. He clapped his hands together, startling the group into attention. "Alright, *listen up*! Everyone grab a seat. Tomorrow's gonna be a big day, and we've got a lot to go over."

The recruits shuffled to their seats as Conner dimmed the lights. He clicked the projector on, and the first slide lit up the screen. The smirking face of Lee Lauren filled the frame, his neon clothing practically glowing, his hair styled with precision.

Conner pointed dramatically at the screen. "*This* guy," he declared, "is the reason we're expecting chaos tomorrow. Everyone's coming to see *him*. His safety is our mission."

Lee Lauren, an influencer who thrived on obnoxious viral stunts and hollow praise from his millions of followers, had carved out a lucrative career flaunting his lifestyle to his young and impressionable fans. His recent ventures included his questionable diet book, 'Vomiting Your Way to a Six-Pack', a scamming cryptocurrency titled 'Lauren's Load', and a new dance track called 'Bacon-Flavored Titties', which he was using to headline his latest DJ sets.

"Alright!" Conner barked, spinning back to face the recruits. "Show of hands - who here is willing to take a *bullet* for Lee Lauren?"

Silence.

The room froze as every recruit avoided eye contact, the absurdity of the question hanging heavy in the air.

Conner's jaw tightened. He cleared his throat. "Okay, maybe that's a big ask. Who here would... take a *kick to the shin* for Lee Lauren?"

The recruits exchanged uneasy glances. Not a single hand went up.

Conner sighed, clearly desperate to salvage the moment. "A *mild* scuffle, then?"

After a long pause, a few hesitant hands raised into the air.

"*There we go!*" Conner said, beaming with pride as though this was a resounding success. He straightened his posture, chest puffed out once again. "That's what I like to see. Dedication. And honestly, I'm not surprised - we hired the best of the best. Or, you know, the best we could afford with such short notice."

A murmur of uncertain agreement rippled through the room as Conner turned back to the screen, preparing to drill them further on their duties.

Conner clicked to the next slide. A cartoonish image of a thug attempting to storm a stage flashed onto the screen. It was drawn like a child's security manual, with exaggerated features and bright colours.

"What do we do in situations like this?" Conner asked, his tone filled with intense seriousness.

The young recruit he'd been bragging to earlier shot his hand up, practically vibrating with enthusiasm. "Go ahead, let's hear it," Conner said, gesturing toward him.

"We elbow him in the face... *hard*!" the recruit said proudly.

The room erupted into applause until they saw Conner shaking his head. "No, no," he said, raising a finger in the air. "We calmly escort the target away from the watching public. Once he's out of sight... we *then* elbow him in the face. *Real hard*!"

This earned even louder applause, with a few enthusiastic whoops thrown in for good measure.

Conner grinned, soaking up the reaction. "Alright, people. Tomorrow's going to be madness out there, but if we stick together and follow my lead, we'll get through it."

The recruits nodded along in agreement, but there was an undercurrent of nervous energy.

Chapter Six

During the early hours of Christmas Eve, Santa's sleep was restless, his subconscious dragging him into the same haunting nightmare it had many times before. The memories came alive with cruel clarity, replaying a Christmas Day from his childhood - one that would etch itself into his soul forever.

He was six years old. Back when he went by the name Sam Clarkson.

The small, cold house was silent, save for the occasional creak of the wind pressing against the rickety windows. The boy sat on the threadbare couch, staring at the blank, broken television screen. It had been smashed weeks ago during one of his mother's violent outbursts, the jagged shards of glass still glinting in the corners of the room like forgotten confetti from a party that never happened.

His stomach growled. He hadn't eaten properly for days.

Outside, the world seemed to sparkle with joy. Snow blanketed the streets, and warm golden light poured from the windows of the neighbours' houses. He pressed his face against the frost-covered windowpane, watching as families passed by, their arms laden with gifts, their laughter bubbling into the cold air. Children skipped along in excitement, holding hands with parents who smiled indulgently.

They were happy. They were loved.

His small fingers curled into fists, and his chest ached with a longing so fierce it felt like it might crack him open. Christmas was supposed to be special, wasn't it? A day of love, of kindness. But in this house, Christmas was just another day to be endured.

And then, as if by magic, a miracle appeared.

Through the haze of his tears and the frost on the glass, he saw a figure approach. Red coat. White beard. A sack slung over his shoulder.

"*Santa!*" he gasped, his heart leaping. "He *didn't* forget me. He was just *late!*"

He scrambled off the couch, flinging open the front door with a surge of excitement he hadn't felt in years. For the first time in his life, hope burned brightly in his chest. Santa had come for *him*.

But as the figure stepped inside, the boy's elation crumbled. The man stumbled, his movements unsteady. The strong stench of alcohol hit the boy like a slap. Santa looked confused, his bleary eyes scanning the room.

"You've got a *kid?*" the man slurred, his words thick and clumsy.

Behind him, his mother appeared, laughing as she leaned against the doorframe. "Oh, don't mind him," she said, waving a hand dismissively. "He won't disturb us. He wouldn't *dare*."

Sam stared at her, his lips trembling as he clung to the fragile remnants of his hope. "Merry Christmas, Mum," he said quietly, his voice barely more than a whisper.

She barely spared him a glance. "It will be," she said, winking at the man, "once I get what's in Santa's sack."

The pair began to stumble toward the stairs, their laughter ringing hollowly in the boy's ears. He watched them go, his small hands clutching the edge of his shirt as tears rushed down his cheeks.

"*I love you*, Mummy," he called out desperately.

No response.

Something inside him snapped. A white-hot anger he didn't understand erupted from his tiny chest, and he roared, "*Why don't you love me?!*"

The words echoed through the house like a thunderclap, freezing his mother in her tracks. She turned, her face contorted with fury, and stomped back down the stairs.

"Because you don't know when to *shut up*!" she snarled. The woman grabbed her boy roughly by the arm, her nails digging into his skin, and dragged him toward the back door.

"Let me go! Please, Mummy, I'm sorry!" he sobbed, but her grip only tightened.

She flung the door open, the icy wind biting into his skin like tiny knives. Without hesitation, she shoved him outside into the snow-covered garden.

"Think about your attitude," she spat. "Maybe I'll let you in when I'm done."

With that, she slammed the door, the sound reverberating through the night like a gunshot.

The boy stood there, his small frame trembling as the cold seeped into his bones. Snowflakes fell gently around him, dusting his hair and eyelashes. His tears froze on his cheeks as he stared at the darkened house, waiting for the door to reopen.

It wouldn't be till the following day when it finally did.

Chapter Seven

Santa awoke from his slumber.

Despite it being Christmas Eve, the familiar spark of joy was gone. Any other year, he'd have leapt out of the bed like a child, heart pounding with excitement, buzzing with anticipation. He used to count down the hours, giddy at the thought of handing out gifts and spreading joy. But today? The magic had vanished, leaving behind only a gnawing emptiness that twisted in his gut.

He groaned as he sat up, the cold biting through the thin, threadbare blanket draped over him. The decrepit home groaned and shivered along with him, the wind howling through the cracked windows like a warning. Normally, he wouldn't even notice the chill. He'd be too wrapped up in the blissful chaos of the season to care. But now, the cold felt different - like it was sinking deeper, into his bones. Into his heart.

His eyes wandered, scanning the decaying room, landing on the collapsed old piano in the corner. The once-grand instrument was now a rotten heap, its keys yellowed and warped, the wood splintering and falling apart. It seemed as broken as his spirit, a sad reflection of what used to be.

And beside the piano sat Mrs. Claus, slumped in her chair, knitting away - at least, in Santa's mind. Her skeletal hands moved delicately, her rotting face contorted into a warm, loving smile. In his twisted vision, she was as lively as ever. She looked up at him, gleaming with affection.

"What's wrong, sweetheart?" she asked, her voice smooth in his hallucination.

Santa sighed, sinking deeper into the bed. "I don't think I want to kill them anymore. Not today," he muttered, his voice heavy with fatigue. "I think… maybe I was overreacting before."

Mrs. Claus tilted her head slightly, her hands still moving in an imaginary rhythm. "What would you like to do instead, dear?"

"...Nothing," Santa replied, his voice dull.

She cocked her head, her expression softening. "You sound depressed, love."

Santa just lay there, staring at the ceiling, feeling the weight of the world pressing down on him. "Maybe," he whispered.

In his warped mind, Mrs. Claus set aside her knitting, rising gracefully from her chair and strolling over to the bed. She sat beside him, her decayed hand stroking his white hair gently. "I know today is going to be very different this year," she murmured, her voice low and sweet. "But that doesn't have to be a bad thing."

He felt her hand cup his cheek, her touch as cold as the air around them. "Come on, love," she whispered. "You can't let this Christmas Eve slip away. You can still make it special..."

Her voice softened and then, slowly, twisted into a melody. The haunting sound seemed to fill the room as she began to sing, her brittle voice echoing with eerie festivity.

> "Oh, it's Christmas Eve, my dear,
> But things are looking dark!
> The sleigh bells aren't a-jingling,
> And there's no snow in the park.
>
> But that's okay, no need to frown,
> We'll make our own festive fun!
> With sharpened blades and wicked grins,
> Yes, it'll be a killer one!"

Santa groaned and rolled over, dragging the tattered pillow over his head. "I don't want to do anything," he mumbled, his voice muffled by the pillow. "No sleigh. No reindeer. No… killing. Not this year."

The song wasn't done. The room, once dull and grey, began to shift. Christmas magic unfolded before his very eyes. The collapsed piano in the corner groaned, its rotten wood creaking as pieces snapped back into place. The yellowed keys straightened, the cracked strings tightened, and soon, the instrument stood upright again, as if it had never fallen into disrepair.

Colours bled into the room like a fever dream, seeping back into the dusty old decorations. The faded tinsel gleamed with an unnatural glow, and the dim Christmas lights flickered back to life, their vibrant colours flooding the space with an almost surreal brightness as if they were at a rock concert. The room pulsed with energy.

Mrs. Claus waltzed over to the newly restored piano. She sat down at the bench, her skeletal fingers hovering over the keys, and with a gleeful grin, she began to play. Each note from the piano echoed through the room, the haunting melody wrapping itself around Santa like a tightening noose.

> "You say you're done, you're out of tricks,
> But dear, you've just begun!
> This year, no toys, no bags of cheer -
> Instead, there will be blood and fear!"

Santa stared at her, transfixed, the macabre tune twisting his thoughts, tugging at the parts of him that still remembered the thrill of Christmas. The melody wormed its way into his mind, refusing to let go.

As if caught up in the strange magic filling the room, he found himself singing too, his voice low and melancholic.

"I'm tired, dear. So tired, dear.

I'm long over the hill.

I've no energy to get out of bed,

Let alone go out and kill."

He looked to the side of him, staring blankly at the bedside table. On it sat a lonely nutcracker, surrounded by broken shells from the night before. He picked one up, absently cracking the shell between his fingers. That's all he wanted to do - crack nuts. To snack away and forget about everything else. The thought of dragging his tired old body through the motions of revenge felt pointless now, like a joke that had lost its punchline.

"What's the point in anything anymore?" he muttered.

Suddenly, the Nutcracker on the table moved, its stiff wooden arms jerking to life. Santa blinked as it grinned up at him, its painted teeth gleaming in the flashing lights. Then, without warning, the Nutcracker too burst into song.

"Don't you see, don't you know,

This Christmas Eve is yours to grow!

Although it may be different now,

Make it better and take a bow."

Santa watched in a daze as more objects in the room began to stir. The garland strung across the walls shimmered, as if woken from a long slumber, and the old stockings hanging at the end of the

47

bed swayed gently to the eerie rhythm of the song. Even the broken ornaments scattered on the floor began to roll about, spinning and bouncing to the haunting tune, as if possessed by the dark holiday magic unfolding around him.

A knock came from the window, and Santa turned in awe. Outside, a group of Elves stood on each other's shoulders,

their grinning faces pressed against the glass. Their sharp, toothy smiles gleamed in the dim light, eyes sparkling with mischief. In unison, they picked up the song, their voices high-pitched yet menacing, carrying the eerie melody forward:

"Take your axe, your sharpest knives,
You'll be carving more than turkey!
They've been naughty, very bad—
It's time for you to go berser...ky?!"

Santa chuckled. The absurdity of it all stirred something deep inside him, a dark spark that had long been buried beneath the bitterness and pain. He hadn't felt this alive in years.

Mrs. Claus, still seated at the piano, slowed the tempo, her bony fingers dancing delicately across the keys. She leaned forward with a sultry grin, her voice low and smooth as it slithered its way into his thoughts:

"They think it's okay to ruin Christmas,
And get away with it!

Not on Santa's watch, oh no,
Their heads he's going to split!"

Her voice deepened, filled with cruel joy, as she continued:

"Cos when you upset Santa,
He's coming on his sled.
He'll come on down your chimney,
And then... well, you will be dead."

With a deep sigh, Santa swung his legs out of bed. The house seemed to hold its breath, the very walls watching, waiting. He stood up slowly, the floor creaking beneath him, and glanced around the room, now bathed in the glow of twisted holiday cheer.

"Well..." he muttered, a twisted grin creeping across his face, "...new traditions, right?"

The entire room seemed to burst into song, the Elves, Mrs. Claus, and even the ornaments on the floor joining in gleefully:

"New traditions, new delight!
On this merry, blood-soaked night!
Sharpened sleighs and screams of fright,
Oh, Christmas Eve will be a sight!"

Santa chuckled louder, the madness bubbling up inside him as he reached for his tattered red coat. The festive spirit around him swelled, the house seeming to hum with his decision, urging him forward, celebrating his choice.

He marched outside, the cold biting at his skin, but it no longer bothered him. The familiar shape of his sleigh stood waiting. In reality, it was nothing more than his battered old Ford Fiesta, rusted and worn, but in his mind, it was his grand sleigh, complete with reindeer snorting in anticipation.

As the music continued to play in his head, Santa climbed into the driver's seat. He gripped the wheel like it was the reins of his mighty sleigh, glancing back one last time at the house. In the window, Mrs. Claus and the Elves waved proudly, their ghoulish faces beaming with excitement.

Maybe Christmas wasn't dead after all - it had simply... *evolved*. The punishment for being extremely naughty was no longer a lump of coal, but something far more sinister. And tonight, the world would discover that grim new reality in the harshest way possible.

Chapter Eight

Santa strolled slowly down the narrow aisles of the DIY store with his shopping cart, his boots scuffing against the dull, grey linoleum floor. This wasn't the Christmas Eve he was used to. Normally, at this time of year, he'd be holding court at the centre of his twinkling Christmas village, children queueing for a chance to sit on his knee, eyes bright with excitement, parents snapping pictures and beaming with pride. But here? He was just another faceless man in a red suit. No one gave him a second glance.

The store was a different kind of chaos.

There were no cheerful carols, no festive greetings exchanged. Just stressed-out shoppers grabbing last-minute items off the shelves with hurried, irritated sighs. The lights buzzed overhead, and the only other sound apart from the clattering of carts was the monotony of the self-checkout machines repeating, "Please place the item in the bagging area."

Santa wandered through the aisles, clutching his tattered sack tighter. It wasn't filled with toys today - no dolls, no trains. Not this time. He was here for something else entirely. His eyes darted to the shelves, scanning for potentially deadly tools.

A few feet ahead, a young girl stood with her mother, who was frantically comparing cans of paint. Santa's heart leapt for a moment.

A child!

He smiled under his beard and approached.

"*Hello there*," he said, his voice jolly, but strained. "Have you been a good little girl this year?"

The girl stared up at him in awe, her eyes wide with wonder. For a brief moment, Santa felt the familiar warmth - the kind that came from knowing a child still believed in the magic of Christmas. Still believed in him. But before the girl could even open her mouth to speak, her mother yanked her away, pulling her close like she was shielding her from some lurking danger.

Santa stood frozen, his outstretched hand slowly falling back to his side. He was used to parents nudging their children forward, encouraging them to approach with wide smiles and excited whispers. But this? This was different. The mother's eyes flashed with suspicion, her body language tense.

A dull ache spread through Santa's chest. His heart sank, the rejection twisting like a knife. Once, children had flocked to him, and parents had trusted him with their most prized possession. Now, he wasn't just unwanted - he was feared.

Santa's fingers twitched, his knuckles cracking as dark, venomous thoughts rushed back to him, suffocating any last trace of the jolly old man he used to be. Kieran - that smug, arrogant prick - was the reason for *all of this*.

Kieran and his cronies treated Santa like a Christmas tree on Boxing Day - used up and tossed to the curb without a second thought.

But no one tosses Santa aside.

Revenge was going to be sweeter than any festive pudding.

His eyes locked onto a nail gun, and his mind instantly spiralled into a dark, vivid fantasy. He didn't just see it - he could *feel* it. Kieran, pinned to the wall, arms splayed wide in a grotesque mockery of the crucifixion. Santa's grip would be firm, unwavering, as he pressed the trigger against Kieran's trembling flesh.

The first nail would drive through his hand, clean and precise.

Kieran would scream, his voice cracking with raw, panicked agony, but Santa would only laugh. That laughter would grow as the second nail tore through the other hand, then the feet, binding Kieran to the wall like a twisted tribute to the man of the season.

It's almost Jesus's birthday, after all, Santa mused, grinning to himself, picturing Kieran's mangled body hanging helplessly. The image filled him with a sick sense of satisfaction.

He moved on, his eyes gleaming as they scanned a display of superglue. His heart raced at the thought of Liz, that self-righteous, holier-than-thou bitch, who strutted around like she was above everyone else. In his mind, he pictured her face - her smug, superior expression twisting into horror as he grabbed her by the hair. He'd slam her face into a pile of shattered Christmas ornaments, the

53

shards embedding themselves into her skin. But that wasn't enough. No, the superglue would ensure the glass stuck deep, bonding her flesh to the sharp edges. She'd scream and struggle, but every movement would only rip her face further apart. The more she fought, the worse it would get, her skin peeling away with every tug.

Santa chuckled to himself, a low, menacing sound, as he grabbed a tube of the glue. It was light, and easy to conceal in his coat pocket. As he moved further down the aisle, his eyes landed on a rack of saws, glinting under the fluorescent lights.

The hacksaw. *Yes.*

Conner, that delusional security guard who thought he was James frickin' Bond. Santa could already see the scene in his head - sneaking up behind Conner, the saw grating slowly across his skin, the teeth of the blade biting in deep but not enough to kill. Not yet. Conner would scream, and thrash, but Santa would take his time. He'd slice through tendons, methodically, rendering the man helpless, leaving him writhing on the cold mall floor. He'd let Conner bleed out slowly, his last sight being Santa's boots stepping away into the flickering Christmas lights.

There was just one last thing santa needed

Santa's breathing quickened, excitement thrumming in his chest as he continued to stalk the aisles, his gaze darting from tool to tool like a predator sizing up its prey. There was just one more thing he needed to complete his mental shopping list, but finding it in the vast labyrinth of the store was proving tricky. As he turned down

54

another row, his eyes fell on a young employee, slumped against the shelves, lazily sniffing glue for a cheap high.

"Excuse me, young man," Santa said, his voice deceptively calm, masking the storm brewing inside him.

The boy blinked, slowly turning to face him, wide-eyed and sluggish. Recognition flickered in his gaze, followed by a smirk. "*I know you*," he said, staring in awe.

"Yes, I'm Santa," he replied with a thin, strained smile.

"Not just *any* Santa," the boy snickered, his eyes gleaming. "*The* Santa. The one from that viral video!"

Santa's face flushed with embarrassment. That *damn* video.

But the boy was unfazed. "Bro, you're a *legend*. Do you have any idea how many customers I wanna slap daily? At least twelve today... within the first hour!"

Santa, eager to steer the conversation away from his disgrace, cleared his throat. "I'm looking for some rope."

"What kind of rope are you after?"

"The kind where I can tie a knot easily... something strong enough so that no one could slip out of it."

For a moment, the boy looked at Santa with a touch of suspicion, his eyes shifting to the collection of deadly tools in the shopping cart. Then, as if the absurdity of it all hit him at once, he burst out laughing.

"*Wow*," the boy chuckled, doubling over. "You're not even hiding the fact that you're about to torture or kill someone. That's... *ballsy*."

Santa opened his mouth, sheepish. "*What*? No. I'm n--"

The boy waved him off, still grinning. "I don't give a shit. Nah, dude, I get it. Do you have any idea how many customers I wanna kill daily? There's been three in the last ten minutes. Right now, you represent pretty much *everyone* that works in retail. You're killing it – *literally*. You're on fire, bruh."

A spark of inspiration flashed in Santa's mind. "Oh,'" he said, his tone suddenly bright. "Do you also happen to sell gasoline?"

"Yeah. Aisle seven."

Santa grinned, his smile unnervingly wide. "Perfect."

Chapter Nine

Santa stood in the dingy public toilet of the DIY store, staring into the cracked, grime-streaked mirror. The buzz of the overhead fluorescent flickered with an unnerving hum, casting a jittery glow over his face. His hand trembled as he held a traditional barber shop razor blade, his reflection glaring back at him, mocking him.

The store worker had recognised him.

He'd been spotted. Others surely would spot him too. The beard *had* to go.

But it wasn't just hair. It was a part of his identity. That beard had been a part of him for three decades, a symbol of his role, his purpose. Each bristle carried the weight of countless memories. thousands of kids had tugged on it, expecting it to be fake, only to light up in awe when they realised it was real.

Now, with each slow, hesitant scrape of his traditional barber razor, it felt like he was erasing his soul. The razor grated against his skin, pulling at the thick white hairs that dropped into the sink like the ashes of a dying fire. Each stroke hurt more than the last, not physically, but in a way that gnawed at the core of who he used to be.

Swipe.

The memory of a wide-eyed child, staring at Santa like he was a rock star - erased.

Swipe.

The look of joy on parents' faces as they watched him speak gently to their kids - erased.

Swipe.

When the final patch of hair fell away, Santa looked up, his bare face reflected in the cracked mirror. The man staring back at him was a stranger. His chin, now exposed, looked weak, vulnerable, naked. He *hated* it. The magic, the essence of Santa, was gone. All that was left was a bitter, broken man, his eyes hollow and sunken.

His breathing quickened as his knuckles gripped the sink. What was he now? What had he become?

Suddenly, the door to the toilet slammed open, shattering Santa's spiralling thoughts. He stiffened, his gaze snapping to the mirror.

It was *him*. That smug, suited asshole who had given him the Tiffany necklace and then crashed into him after he was thrown out of the Mall.

With a phone glued to his ear, the man gave Santa a quick, dismissive glance. "Fucking *weirdo*," he muttered under his breath before striding into a cubicle.

Santa's stomach churned with rage, but the man kept talking, his voice dripping with arrogance. "No, *not you*, babe," he continued, the smirk clear in his tone. "I was talking to some Hills Have Eyes creepy looking incest motherfucker."

Santa's ears burned as the man kept babbling. "Yeah, babe, I know. But let's be realistic here - I can't ditch the wife and kids on *Christmas Day*, you know how it is - but don't worry. Boxing Day, I'll make an excuse to get out of the house. Then it's just you and me. Can't wait to bend you over again. God, I miss that ass."

Santa's vision blurred with a seething rage. His grip on the razor tightened, his knuckles white with the tension. This piece of filth was laughing about cheating - at *Christmas*, no less! The hypocrisy, the sheer disrespect, felt like a slap to everything the season stood for. Family. Kindness. *Love*.

The anger boiled up inside Santa, hotter and more intense than ever. This man - this scumbag - was everything wrong with the world. Selfish. Cruel. Unfaithful.

He stared at the razor in his hand. He knew what he had to do.

He couldn't let this one go. Not this time.

With a roar that echoed through the small, tiled room, Santa stormed forward, kicking open the cubicle door with a force that splintered the wood, sending it crashing against the wall.

The man looked up, eyes wide with terror, the phone slipping from his hand. "What the fu--"

"You're *very naughty*!" Santa bellowed, his voice booming like thunder in the confined space. Before the man could react, Santa plunged the razor into his throat with a brutal, savage thrust.

The sound was wet and sickening, the blade slicing through skin and muscle. Blood sprayed from the wound, splattering across the cubicle walls and floor, coating Santa's hands and arms in thick, dark red. The man gurgled, his eyes bulging in shock as he clutched at his throat, trying to stop the blood from pouring out.

But Santa didn't stop.

He yanked the blade free and slashed again, this time deeper, severing the man's windpipe.

A fountain of blood erupted from the gash, spraying Santa's face, but the red suit hid it well. The victim kicked his legs wildly whilst sitting on the toilet, gasping and choking for air. His body convulsed as blood poured from his mouth, bubbling and thick.

Santa stood over him, breathing heavily, his chest heaving with every laboured breath.

The man was still twitching, barely alive, his hands slick with blood as he desperately tried to stem the flow.

Santa grinned, his eyes gleaming with satisfaction. "*Naughty...* so *very naughty.*"

With a final, savage plunge, Santa drove the razor deep into the man's chest, twisting it as he felt the blade grind against bone. The man's body jerked one last time, a final, pitiful gasp escaping his lips before he slumped lifelessly.

Blood pooled beneath him, soaking into the tiled floor, thick and dark.

Santa wiped the blade on the man's shirt, the sticky blood leaving smears across the fabric.

The door burst open with a bang, the noise sending a shock through Santa's body. For a split second, panic consumed him - was this the end before it had even begun? His eyes darted to the entrance, bracing for security, cops, or worse.

But instead, it was the young DIY store worker from earlier, now in his regular clothes. The kid froze at the sight of the bloodied mess, his eyes widening in shock. For a tense moment, they stared at each other. Then, slowly, the boy raised his hands, palms out, stepping back cautiously. "I saw *nothing*," he said, voice trembling but defiant. "Besides, that guy's a prick. He's in here all the time, treating everyone like shit. You know how many times I've thought about doing this to him myself? Twice! Today!"

With a final glance, the kid backed away, vanishing from sight as quickly as he'd appeared.

Santa exhaled sharply, a wave of relief washing over him, but he knew the clock was ticking. The next person through that door would likely not be so forgiving. It was time to move. Fast.

Chapter Ten

Kieran stormed through Merryvale Shopping Mall, his jaw clenched and shoulders stiff under the weight of mounting frustration. What should have been a day of bustling shoppers and ringing tills had devolved into a different kind of chaos, thanks to Lee Lauren - the social media influencer who had turned the mall into a madhouse.

Teenagers were everywhere, forming dense, chaotic clusters. They swarmed near the stage and around life-size posters of Lee, their manic energy thick in the air. Some were kissing his grinning image, smearing lipstick on the glossy paper like he was the second coming. Others sobbed theatrically, clutching their phones and live-streaming the frenzy to friends who hadn't managed to secure a spot.

One girl crouched beside a display of Christmas ornaments, eyes wild with determination, as she discreetly peed into an empty water bottle, unwilling to give up her prime viewing spot. Kieran gagged and turned away, his stomach twisting in revulsion.

None of these kids were spending a single penny. They weren't browsing the shops or buying something to eat; they were just loitering, taking up space, creating mess after mess. They soaked up the festive atmosphere without contributing a thing, and Kieran could feel the rage bubbling just beneath the surface.

As he stepped around a group of girls belting out Lee Lauren's absurd hit, "Bacon-Flavoured Titties," he caught sight of the day's warm-up act climbing onto the stage. It was Tammy and Tommy, known as The Thompson Twins, a painfully mediocre sibling duo who'd somehow risen to fleeting fame by coming seventh on the hit TV show "You're a Bit Shit" - a competition to find the UK's worst singers.

Tammy, with her hair styled like an overambitious Christmas tree, grabbed the mic and grinned at the crowd. "Who's excited to see *Lee Lauren*?" she chirped.

The crowd erupted into deafening cheers.

Tommy, wearing a sequined blazer that looked like it belonged to a Las Vegas pawn shop, added, "He'll be on stage soon, but first, we're The Thompson Twins! Let us *entertain you*!"

The siblings launched into the butchering of a Robbie Williams classic, their off-key warbling making Kieran's eye twitch.

In the first verse of the song are the lyrics, "Shake your arse, come over here… now *scream*!" At this point The Taylor Twins held out their microphones, encouraging the audience to scream.

Nobody screamed.

Kieren quickened his pace, desperate to escape the noise, when a different sound cut through the chaos - something sharper and more alarming. It was a boy's distressed cry.

The Mall owner snapped his head toward the noise, instantly spotting the source. One of Conner's rent-a-guards had pinned a teenage boy to the tiled floor near the food court. The guard's face was twisted with righteous fury as he wrestled the boy's arms behind his back. "*No vaping!*" the guard screamed, as though he were busting a major drug dealer instead of a scrawny kid whose only crime was puffing out a cloud of cherry-scented smoke.

The boy squirmed and whimpered, his eyes wide with terror. Around them, a crowd of onlookers gathered, some laughing, others filming the incident on their phones. Kieran felt a knot tighten in his gut. Fantastic. Another PR disaster to pile on top of everything else.

Grabbing his walkie-talkie, he pressed the button so hard his knuckles whitened. "Conner!" he barked, his voice sharp with anger. "Get your damn recruits in line! One of them has just assaulted *another* kid!"

No response.

Of course not. Conner was probably too busy posturing as the mall's resident action hero to deal with the mess his goons were creating.

Kieran rubbed his temples, his patience wearing thin. He glanced toward the glowing green exit sign in the distance, beckoning him like a beacon of salvation. If he could just make it there, he might steal a few precious moments of peace. The crisp bite of cold air, the stillness of the outside world, and the calming embrace of a cigarette were all he wanted. Just a moment to breathe before diving back into the madness.

He wasted no time weaving through the crowds. Just a minute or two, and then--

"Mr. Poole!"

He winced as a journalist materialised out of nowhere, blocking his path. The man had a voice recorder in hand, and his urgent tone made it clear he wasn't going to be brushed off easily.

"Paul Bellow here, from the Comfy Pillow Podcast," the man said with the air of someone expecting recognition.

Kieran blinked. "There's a podcast about comfy pillows?"

"There's a podcast about everything," Paul replied smoothly. "Turns out that pretty much *everyone* loves a comfy pillow!"

"Fair enough," Kieran muttered, already feeling the conversation veering off course. "What do you want?"

"A quick interview," Paul said, his voice suddenly serious. "You seem a bit out of your depth hosting Lee Lauren here today. Would you agree?"

Kieran straightened up, bristling. "What makes you say that?"

Paul gave a nonchalant shrug. "Oh, just a few, uh, amateurish choices I've noticed. Like your security frisking everyone at the entrance to confiscate weapons - while there are at least three stores in here open *right now* selling guns. One of them has even got a 70% off sale going."

Kieran felt his face flush with embarrassment. "My team knows what they're doing. It's going to be a great day. As you can imagine, I don't really have time to talk right now."

Paul wasn't done. He leaned forward, a sly grin on his face. "One last question. It's real important."

Kieran sighed. "*Go on.*"

"What's your preferred pillow filling? Feather or cotton?"

Kieran stared at him, caught between disbelief and fury. "I... I don't have time for this," he said, shaking his head as he sidestepped the persistent reporter.

He picked up his pace, determined to make it to the exit, but peace was not on the cards. Before he could get far, a familiar voice called out.

"*Kieran!*"

Liz marched over, her phone pointed at him like a weapon. Her eyes gleamed with a manic energy that only meant one thing: disaster.

"I need you to do a quick dance for the camera," she said, breathless with urgency.

Kieran froze, his brow furrowing in disbelief. "*What*? Right *now*?!"

"We're getting hammered with bad media attention as we speak," she rattled off, the words tumbling out in a rush. "People are saying we're completely out of our depth having Lee Lauren here, and it's going to end in total disaster!"

"Yeah, I've already heard that from the Comfy Pillow Podcast," Kieran said, deadpan. "But I don't give a shit what they think."

"*Comfy Pillow Podcast is here*?" Liz's eyes widened in genuine horror. "*Fuck.* It's worse than I thought. They've got tens of millions of listeners! And they don't fuck about with their journalism – proper *hard-hitting* stuff. We need to show them... no, we need to show *everyone* that *everything* is under control. A quick, silly dance from senior management will spread some holiday cheer, drown out the bad press, and prove we're not, as reported, in crisis mode."

Kieran just stared at her, speechless. Any hope of reasoning with her was gone. With a heavy sigh, he gritted his teeth, forcing a tight, awkward smile that felt faker than the plastic Christmas tree next to them.

"*Fine*," he muttered, already feeling his dignity slipping away.

He raised his arms in a stiff, awkward attempt at a dance, shuffling his feet like a wind-up toy on its last few cranks. Liz grinned, clearly thrilled as she recorded his humiliating performance for social media. Meanwhile, Kieran could feel his soul withering with every uncoordinated step. Teens nearby were already pulling out their own phones, filming him and snickering behind their screens.

Each second felt like an eternity, his skin prickling with embarrassment. His forced smile was starting to ache, and the weight of every mocking stare from the crowd settled heavily on him. Finally, he let his arms drop, his grin dissolving into a hard, bitter scowl.

"That's enough," he snapped, his voice edged with exhaustion and frustration.

Liz, looking like she'd just won the lottery, lowered her phone, satisfied with the footage. "That was great! We'll post it with some Christmas music and a festive filter. Trust me, it'll turn things around and th--."

Kieran was already walking away, storming past the Christmas village at the centre of the mall. He spotted Lord Steeler, the pompous fill-in Santa, looking frazzled in his ill-fitting costume.

A young boy was standing in front of him, clutching his stomach, his face a pale green. The inevitable happened in a matter of seconds - the kid vomited all over Lord Steeler's lap, splattering his velvet Santa suit in an explosion of half-digested candy and hot chocolate.

Steeler jumped up from his throne, ripping off his fake beard, his face red with fury. "How am I supposed to work under *these conditions*?!" he bellowed, his voice echoing through the mall. "I played background inmate #15 in The Shawshank Redemption, dammit! This is a *disgrace!*"

Kieran groaned, pulling his walkie-talkie from his pocket again. "*Conner!*" he barked into the device, "Santa's losing his damn mind! Sort it out!"

No response. Just static.

With a sigh of growing frustration, Kieran pushed onward, eyes locked on the glowing green exit sign - his freedom.

As he passed a sweet shop, a piercing alarm rang out, immediately followed by the sight of one of Conner's rent-a-guards running out of the store, before tripping over himself and flying to the ground. The impact sent a shower of M&M's he'd been clinging onto, creating a slippery minefield beneath the feet of unsuspecting shoppers.

It was a scene straight out of a slapstick comedy - people stumbling, sliding, and falling as they tried to navigate the sugary disaster. Bags flew, curses were muttered, and shoppers tumbled into each other like dominoes.

Kieran stopped dead, watching the mayhem unfold in disbelief. His hand instinctively went to his walkie-talkie.

"*Conner*!" he barked louder than before, the frustration evident in his voice. "Where the fuck are you?!"

Silence. Again.

He clenched the device, half-ready to throw it. But no - this wasn't his problem. Not right now. Not until he got his much-needed fix of nicotine.

Determined to finally escape the madness, Kieran finally reached the exit, shoving the door open with such force that it rattled in its frame. Cool air washed over him like a balm, and he fumbled for a cigarette, desperate for a moment of peace. But just as he pulled one out and placed it between his lips, reality delivered another blow: no lighter.

"*Fuck*!" he growled, his anger flaring up again.

As if the universe had a cruel sense of humour, a flicker of flame appeared right in front of his face.

Kieran blinked, momentarily startled, before sighing with relief. "Thanks," he muttered to the stranger, leaning in to light his cigarette.

He didn't bother to really look at the man. He was just some random guy offering a light.

Unbeknownst to Kieran, the man holding the lighter was actually none other than the very Santa he had fired earlier that week. Only this time, Santa was unrecognisable. Beardless, disguised, blending in among the holiday shoppers.

Santa's smile was anything but jolly now. There was no twinkle in his eye, no hint of good-natured cheer. His grin, twisted and malicious, was more akin to the Grinch's - only far darker. He wasn't here to steal Christmas.

He was here to burn the motherfucker down!

Chapter Eleven

Liz sat alone in her office, the faint hum of electronics filling the air like the background score to a nightmare. The glow of the monitors illuminated her face, casting long, ghostly shadows across the walls. Each screen was alive with the chaotic chatter of social media, a relentless flood of brutal headlines, mocking memes, and shaky video clips documenting the ongoing disaster at Merryvale Shopping Mall.

Her carefully curated attempt to save their reputation was unravelling in real time, each comment slicing into her confidence like a dagger:

"Merryvale Mall is a joke. My grandma's funeral had better vibes!"

"WTF is with the security at Merryvale? Looks like bring your kids to work day!"

"Lee Lauren is playing here?! Seriously?!! Merryvale is a shit hole!"

Liz's trembling fingers scrolled frantically through her phone, desperate for a glimmer of positivity. Anything to cling to. But there was nothing - just an endless stream of toxicity.

Her heart pounded erratically, the edges of her vision dimming with every scathing remark. This event had been her chance to shine, to prove herself as the mastermind behind Merryvale's resurgence. Instead, it was becoming her tombstone

"*No, no, no,*" she whispered hoarsely, leaning closer to the monitors, her breath fogging the screens. I can fix this. I *have* to fix this "

A new notification popped up, dragging her attention like a hook to the flesh. She clicked on the video without thinking, dread twisting her stomach.

It was Kieran.

It was the footage of him dancing, his arms flailing awkwardly. A group of teens jeered and howled with laughter in the background.

"*Cringe,*" one of them sneered.

Liz's face burned with shame. She slammed a button, killing the monitor. She turned to another screen and another, shutting them off in rapid succession, each one silencing a mocking voice.

Finally, the room was almost completely dark, except for the faint light coming from the single remaining monitor. She reached out to kill the last screen when a faint movement in its reflection stopped her cold.

Her breath hitched.

A figure stood behind her, shadowed but unmistakable.

Slowly, she turned her head, her blood running ice cold.

Santa!

But not the jolly, bearded mall Santa from days ago. No, this was something else entirely. He was stripped of the beard, his pale face gaunt and angular, his piercing blue eyes burning with cold fury. Yet despite the transformation, Liz recognised him instantly. "Y-you," she stammered, her voice cracking.

Santa's lips curled into a smile.

"I'm impressed that you recognise me, Liz," he rumbled, his voice low and menacing, like thunder rolling in the distance.

Her knees trembled. "You... you shouldn't be here."

"Oh, but I *should*," he said, stepping closer towards her, his boots thudding against the floor. "This was my home - where I belonged. You stole it from me."

The walkie-talkie on her desk crackled to life, jolting her.

"Lee Lauren is in the building! I repeat, Lee Lauren is officially in the building!" chirped a cheerful staff member:

Liz's hand shot out, fumbling for the device. She clutched it like a lifeline, "H-hel--"

Santa's hand lashed out, grabbing the device and wrenching it from her grasp. His grip crushed it, the plastic cracking with a sharp snap, before he flung it to the floor.

His grin widened as he loomed over his prey. "Before you run off to your precious Lee Lauren, why don't we give you a starring role first?"

From his coat, he pulled out his own phone, the screen glowing as he pointed it at her. With a mocking flourish, he hit record.

"Dance for me, Liz," he commanded, his tone sharp.

Liz recoiled, her back pressing against her chair. "What is this?" she whispered, her voice trembling. "No. I don't want to."

Santa's smile twisted into a sneer. "All those people in your shitty little videos... I'm pretty sure they didn't want to dance either," he said, his voice dripping with venom. "All those people you *humiliated* for engagement. They looked truly dead inside, desperate for it to be over. But that didn't matter to you, as long as the clicks rolled in."

He reached into his coat again and pulled out a knife. The blade gleamed under the cold light of the monitor.

"*Dance*," he repeated, his voice now a growl.

Liz's legs felt like lead, but she rose, trembling. "Okay. Sure," she said, terrified.

She swayed awkwardly, raising her arms in a feeble attempt to obey.

"*That's it?*" Santa taunted, stepping closer. The blade hovered near her face. He used it to lift the corner of her mouth into a grotesque smile. "Show me the *passion*, Liz. And c'mon, smile for your audience."

Tears streamed down her face as she tried to shuffle faster, her movements jerky and desperate.

Without warning, Santa plunged the knife into her thigh.

Liz screamed, collapsing as blood gushed from the wound, staining her skirt and pooling on the floor.

"Dance *better*!" Santa roared, twisting the blade. "Use your legs! *Use* them or *lose* them!"

Liz sobbed as she clawed at the desk, dragging herself upright. She shuffled, her injured leg dragging behind her, blood smearing across the floor. Each movement sent fresh agony ripping through her body.

"*Pathetic*," Santa spat, kicking her wounded leg. Liz collapsed again, her hands slipping in the crimson puddle.

She whimpered. "*Please. I'm sorry...*"

Santa crouched beside her, his face inches from hers. His icy blue eyes bored into her soul. "Where was this empathy the other day?" he whispered.

Santa jabbed the knife into Liz's chest.

Her screams filled the room as blood sprayed across the walls, splattering the flickering monitor.

"With what little energy you have left… *dance*!" Santa growled, his voice laced with mocking amusement. "Your life literally depends on it."

The phone's camera lens glinted as it continued to record, capturing every agonising second of Liz's torment.

Liz trembled, forcing herself to move despite the unbearable pain. Her shoulders swayed weakly, a pathetic mimicry of a dance. Blood oozed from her wounds, her body faltering with every strained effort. Each movement slowed further, her strength ebbing away like the life pooling beneath her.

She collapsed at last, her trembling form crumpling into the crimson lake surrounding her. Her limbs twitched, spasms of fading energy, until they stilled entirely.

Santa crouched beside her motionless body, his shadow looming over her like a predator savouring its kill. He reached out with the tip of his blade, tilting her head to face him. Her eyes stared into nothingness, lifeless and vacant.

Santa ended the recording with a deliberate click.

"*Perfect*," he murmured, his voice dripping with satisfaction. "You're going to be *famous*, Liz. You're going to get *so many* views."

Standing, he tucked the phone back into his coat, his boots crunching against the shattered remnants of the walkie-talkie as he turned to walk toward the door.

Behind him, the room fell silent save for the faint hum of electronics.

The lone monitor still flickered, its glow casting eerie shadows across Liz's lifeless body. The endless scroll of social media continued, oblivious to the horror that had unfolded:

"Whoever planned this trainwreck should be fired. Or worse!"

76

Chapter Twelve

The Green Room of Merryvale Shopping Mall was really just the staff break room with delusions of grandeur. It smelled faintly of stale coffee and Lynx Africa, with a couple of sagging couches that had seen better days. Someone had tried to class them up with new pillows, but they did little to hide the worn-out cushions beneath. The walls were plastered with faded posters from mall events long gone. One particularly haunting image was of the "Meet Mickey Mouse" experience, featuring a knockoff costume so bad you could see the person's human eyes peering through the mesh of the mouse's dead stare. Above it, a laminated HR sign hung at an awkward angle, sternly proclaiming: "A polite reminder: Sexual harassment will not be tolerated at the staff Christmas party. Especially you, Dave."

Conner stood in the middle of the room, bouncing lightly on his heels like a kid trying to be picked during gym class. He was desperate to impress the "big-time" influencer sprawled across from him. Lee Lauren, lazily perched on the arm of one of the battered couches, was bathed in the dim glow of his phone, scrolling through his feed with a look of detached boredom. To him, Conner was nothing more than an irritation - just background noise, an unwelcome distraction from the endless stream of likes and comments flooding his screen.

The security guard cleared his throat loudly, inching closer, desperate for attention. "So," he said awkwardly. "How long did it take you to learn the art of DJing?"

"The *art*?" Lee Lauren laughed. "I press play on an hour-long track previously mixed for me whilst, now and then, pumping my arms in the air."

"Cool," Conner replied. "Ya know... I've always thought about getting into private security. Real high-end stuff."

Lee didn't even glance up. He mumbled something vaguely affirmative, which to Conner sounded like encouragement. He pressed on, excitement bubbling up.

"Yeah, so, if you ever need a guy who can handle pretty much anything, I'm your man. I once killed a guy with nothing more than... a rubber chicken and a stapler."

That got Lee's attention. He paused mid-scroll, finally looking up with an expression somewhere between confusion and disbelief. "*Really?*" he asked flatly, his voice dripping with sarcasm.

Conner puffed out his chest, a self-satisfied grin spreading across his face as he leaned into his story. "Oh yeah. Guy came at me outta nowhere so I had to grab whatever was closest to me. Bam! Rubber chicken to the face, then I finished him off with a stapler. Didn't stand a chance."

Lee's eyes flicked over to the coffee table where a rubber chicken and a stapler just so happened to be sat, right next to a sad-looking platter of crackers. His eyebrows shot up. "You're not just saying that because a rubber chicken and stapler is sitting right there, are you?"

Conner's grin faltered. "Uh, no," he stammered, trying to recover. "That's just a... coincidence."

"*Right,*" Lee snorted, clearly unimpressed. "What I don't see on that table though, is my huge bowl of M&M's." He folded his arms, glaring at Conner like a teacher who'd caught a kid without his homework. "It clearly states in my contract that I don't do shit until I've had my M&M's."

"Yeah, course!" Conner said, his voice going up a little too high. "One of my officers is on the case. He should be here... any minute now."

Lee crossed his arms like a toddler on the verge of a tantrum. "He better be, Kindergarten Cop, or I don't go on stage." The celebrity returned to his phone with the threat lingering in the air like a bad smell.

Conner stood there, trying to suppress the growing panic bubbling up inside him. He could already feel the weight of the situation slipping through his fingers, but he had no choice but to wait for the M&M's to appear. Surely his team could handle that task at least.

Chapter Thirteen

Backstage of the mall's Winter Wonderland, the grotto's cheer was a thin mask over its grim reality. Costumes sagged limply on wire hangers, their colours dulled by years of use and disrepair. As for the rest of the room - the once-glittering space had become a shrine not to holiday magic but to the ego of Lord Steeler. The walls, once adorned with the joyful faces of children meeting Santa, were now plastered with framed relics of Steeler's so-called acting "triumphs." Faded headshots, glossy set photos, and plaques boasting titles such as "Best Tryer of the Performance" and "Most Dedicated Extra – 1994" lined the space.

Lord Steeler stood before a cracked mirror surrounded by a string of flickering holiday lights, their glow barely masking the peeling paint and dust around them. He dabbed at a stubborn stain on the red velvet of his shoulder where a child's sugary vomit clung like an unwelcome badge of honour. His exasperated breaths came in tight, frustrated huffs.

"I was background fisherman #8 in Forrest Gump, for Christ's sake," he muttered to his reflection. "Why am I here, doing *this*? I'm better than this!"

His gaze shifted to the wall of pitiful accolades, their once-shiny metallic paint now chipped and peeling to reveal the cheap plastic beneath. The sight only deepened the pit of resentment in his chest. Sighing with a heaviness that seemed to reverberate through the room, Steeler took a careful sip of his warm lemon water. The steam curled into the dim air. He had relied on this concoction many times before, its tang soothing his throat and allowing him to belt out his performances without faltering.

This time, though, there was an unfamiliar bitterness, a sharp edge that made him pause. He frowned, eyes narrowing as a sudden wave of drowsiness washed over him, creeping through his veins like poison. The room tilted, and the lines of garland and costumes blurred, bleeding into one another. Panic clenched his chest as he struggled to find his footing.

"What's... happening?" Steeler's voice came out a weak slur, his tongue thick and sluggish. He reached desperately for the sink, but his trembling fingers barely brushed the porcelain before his legs gave out. He collapsed to the cold, hard floor, head lolling to the side, eyes wide with confusion as his body refused to obey him.

A flicker of movement drew Steeler's gaze, his eyes struggling to focus through the haze. From behind the rack of tattered elf costumes, a figure emerged, stepping into the dim glow cast by a failing string of holiday lights.

Santa - the "real" Santa - stood before him.

In that moment, Steeler's muddled mind clung to hope. Maybe this strange figure was here to help, a saviour to pull him back from the creeping darkness. He reached out with a trembling hand, desperation etched into the lines of his face. He tried to call for help, to plead, but all that escaped was a ragged, strangled croak.

Santa took another step forward, eyes fixed on Steeler with an unsettling, feverish gleam. In his hand, the light caught on the jagged edge of a rusted saw, its teeth glistening with grim anticipation.

Steeler's eyes widened in pure terror as they locked onto the deadly tool. "No... plea..." he stammered, the words crumbling on his thick, sluggish tongue. His body remained limp, muscles useless against whatever drug coursed through his veins. Frantically, his gaze darted around the room, taking in the scattered pieces of his past - the set photos, framed awards, glossy headshots - now reduced to a meaningless audience for his final, unwelcome act.

Santa said nothing as he approached even closer, his movements deliberate, almost ritualistic. He raised the saw and placed it on the crown of Steeler's scalp. The first bite of the teeth into flesh was sharp and immediate, a red-hot lance of pain that sent Steeler's eyes rolling back as a strangled, wet groan tore from his throat. The saw screeched against bone, the noise mingling with the screams of teenagers waiting to meet Lee Lauren.

Steeler's blood gushed in thick rivulets, sliding down his face and pooling on the grimy floor, soaking the scattered photos of past Santa visits. The saw continued its grisly path, slicing through skin, hair, and the skull with mechanical determination. Santa worked without flinching, the muscles in his arm tensing and releasing in a steady rhythm. The room stank of copper and sweat, the metallic tang thick enough to coat the tongue.

Tears mingled with blood on Steeler's cheeks as the room spun and the agony overwhelmed him. Each stroke of the saw sent spasms through his body, his muscles jerking with the raw, electric shock of it. The once-proud awards around them now seemed like cruel spectators, the grinning photos mocking him in his torment.

Finally, with a sickening squelch, Santa completed the circle, lifting the crown of Steeler's scalp free like a grotesque cap. Blood pulsed from the exposed skull, glistening under the erratic light.

Santa leant across into the costumes to grab his hidden true prize - an already loaded nail gun.

Positioning the tangle of bloody grey hair over Steeler's trembling face, Santa pressed the first nail against his temple. The click-thunk of the gun was followed by a sharp snap as the nail drove home, puncturing skin and scraping bone. Blood spurted from the wound, soaking the makeshift beard.

More nails followed in rapid succession, each impact ringing out like gunshots in the silent room. They punctured Steeler's cheeks, and his jaw, embedding deep into the tender flesh and sinew. With each thud, Steeler's body jerked weakly, the pain now a red tide that blurred the edges of consciousness.

The makeshift beard, now nailed firmly in place, was soaked with dark, arterial blood, strands of grey matted together and tinged red. Santa stood back, his work complete. He touched the beard lightly, nodding in approval."

"Now you look the part," he muttered, his voice rough but satisfied.

Chapter Fourteen

A sudden, frantic pounding rattled the Green Room door, each hit landing with a force that made both Conner and Lee jump. The sharp, desperate sound was so relentless that it drowned out the muffled chaos of the crowd beyond the walls. Conner's stomach flipped as his gaze darted to the door.

"What the hell?" Lee muttered, his usual lazy disdain replaced with genuine unease. For once, his gaze had peeled away from his phone.

"Time to prove yourself, Kindergarten Cop," Lee sneered, his voice dripping with mockery. But Conner caught it - the slight tremor beneath the bravado, the way Lee's hand twitched as he shoved his phone into his jacket pocket.

The security guard squared his shoulders and tried to steady his breath, but his heart was pounding as loud as the assault on the door. Was this it? The moment where he, Conner, finally got to show he was more than just a glorified babysitter?

The door rattled under another thunderous blow. With shaking hands, Conner reached for the handle, muttering to himself under his breath: You've got this. You're the protector. The shield. The—

The second he cracked the door open, the barrier burst inward, nearly taking him off his feet as three members of the security team tumbled into the room like bowling pins. They hit the sticky tile floor in a tangled heap, gasping and groaning.

"What the hell is going on?" Conner yelped, his attempt at authority falling apart as his voice cracked with panic.

The guards were a mess. Their uniforms were dishevelled, sweat staining the collars and underarms. One of them had bright red scratches streaked across his cheek, raw and angry, like he'd been attacked by a swarm of feral cats. Another clutched his side, wheezing for breath, his radio hanging by a frayed cord from his belt. He croaked breathlessly, "The fans. They're… *crazy.*"

Lee stepped forward, his posture exuding the indignant impatience of a man used to being served on a platter. "Well?" he snapped, crossing his arms and leaning against the doorframe. "Did one of you bring my M&M's? Or am I going to have to get you all fired?"

One of the guards raised a trembling hand, fumbling inside his blazer. He pulled something from his jacket with the solemnity of a knight presenting a sacred relic - a crinkled, slightly crushed bag of M&M's.

"*Finally!*" Lee barked, snatching the bag with a level of desperation that matched the pounding from moments before. He tore it open and shoved a handful into his mouth, crunching loudly. "You people are unbelievable," he muttered, spraying half-chewed candy onto the floor as he chewed.

"Are you okay?" Conner asked the guards.

"No," one of them wheezed. "It's like a battleground out there."

"Yeah, I'm like a god to them," Lee explained through a mouthful of chocolate. "Alright, let's get this appearance over with so I can get out of this dump," he continued, already heading for the door.

Conner straightened, his chest puffing out. This was his moment, his chance to prove he could lead. "Okay, team," he said, his voice cracking slightly but laced with enthusiasm. "Let's—"

"Actually," Lee cut him off, turning back with a smirk that was as condescending as it was infuriating. "I think I'll be fine with these guys." He gestured to the battered trio of battered guards. "You should... stay here."

Conner's face fell, his hopeful grin slipping away like a deflated balloon. "Well... I would feel more comfortable if I w—"

But Lee was already out the door, the other guards stumbling after him like soldiers being marched to their doom.

Conner stood frozen, the rejection stinging worse than he'd expected. His gaze dropped to the floor - and that's when he spotted them.

The M&M's.

"Oh," Conner said softly to himself, his eyes filling with tears that were equal parts heartbreak and determination. "Of course. He wants me to protect his candy. Well…" He straightened, clutching the bag to his chest as if it were the crown jewels. "I won't let him down!"

He turned, pacing back to the tiny couch in the corner with renewed purpose. This was his job now. This was his moment.

"Don't worry, M&M's," he whispered, staring at the door with steely resolve. "I'll protect you."

Chapter Fifteen

The Green Room felt oppressively silent as Conner paced, his breath shallow and uneven. He clutched the bag of M&M's tightly, more for comfort at this point than any sense of duty.

Deep down, Conner knew the truth. He had annoyed Lee Lauren. The dismissive celebrity had encouraged him to remain here to create distance - to sideline him like some irritating child who didn't know when to stop talking. The realisation stung, and Conner's pacing grew faster, more erratic, as if the movement could somehow push away his doubts.

The door suddenly creaked open, and Conner froze mid-step. For one hopeful moment, he allowed himself to believe it might be Lee Lauren having a change of heart. Just maybe the crowds were too overwhelming. Maybe he realised he needed Conner's expertise.

Instead, it was Santa.

His massive frame loomed in the doorway. The light from the hallway seemed to vanish behind him, swallowed up by his imposing presence.

His eyes burned with an intensity that froze Conner in place, a storm of emotion swirling just beneath their surface.

Conner tried to swallow the lump in his throat and forced a smile. "Uh, hey, buddy. This area is for staff only. Are you lost or something?"

Santa's voice was low, deliberate. "Very much so. That tends to happen once your purpose is taken from you. You become lost. Broken. *Angry*."

Conner blinked, his confusion plain. "Okay. Uh, how did you get past security?"

Santa stepped fully into the room, his boots clicking ominously against the floor. As he moved closer, Santa pointed to a cheap plastic toy cop badge clipped to his chest.

Conner exhaled sharply, his nerves momentarily abated. "Oh," he laughed. "You're one of us. Sorry, I didn't recognise you."

Santa didn't respond. He just kept walking, closing the distance between them one measured step at a time.

Conner's nerves slowly surged back as he tried to fill the silence. "Y'know, uh, you should probably be manning the stage or something. The performance starts soon. Mr. Lauren's gonna be needi--"

"I'm not here for Lee Lauren," Santa interrupted, his voice as sharp as a knife.

Conner blinked. "Okay... so... what's up?"

"I was up," Santa said, his tone almost conversational. "About three feet in the air, if I recall correctly. When you threw me out of the mall."

The words hit Conner like a slap. His stomach dropped, his mind racing to connect the dots.

His eyes widened. "It's... *you*."

"It is."

"The pervert who was dry-humping the mannequin a few months back!"

Santa's expression flickered with confusion and outrage. "*What? No!* It's *me! Santa!*"

"*Lord Steeler?*"

Santa's patience snapped. He roared, his voice filling the room and reverberating in Conner's chest. "No! The *real* Santa! The one who brought joy to this mall for three decades. The one who sacrificed *everything*, only to be tossed aside like garbage!'

The full weight of recognition hit Conner like a train. "The Santa we fired."

Santa's smirk returned, darker than before. "*There* it is."

Conner took a shaky step back, bumping into the edge of the coffee table. His voice wavered. "Okay, so you're mad. I get it. But why are you here?"

Santa leaned in, his voice dropping to a chilling whisper. "Justice."

Without warning, Santa lunged, pulling a knife from his coat. The blade glinted under the fluorescent light, streaked with something dark and sticky. Conner stumbled backwards, panic flooding his veins. His hand shot into his belt holster, yanking out a gun.

"Stay *back*!" Conner shouted, his voice cracking with fear.

But Santa's laughter filled the room, rich and mocking, "Who are you kidding?" Santa sneered, his eyes gleaming with madness. "We both know that's a *toy*."

Conner's face twisted in panic as he looked down at the plastic gun in his hands, its bright orange tip a glaring reminder of his helplessness. "*Fuck*," he muttered, before frantically grabbing at the nearest objects on the coffee table - a stapler and rubber chicken.

Santa tilted his head, a twisted grin spreading across his face. "Err... *okay*."

Conner swung the rubber chicken with all his might, its squeaky protests echoing comically in the room. The absurdity of the sound made Santa chuckle hysterically. The toy was swung again, and again, its hollow squeaks growing desperate as if the chicken itself was begging for mercy.

Santa's laughter stopped abruptly after the third strike.

He snatched the chicken mid-swing, yanking it from Conner's hand. "Okay, enough games," he said, his face darkening and his eyes gleaming with unholy rage.

Then Santa moved.

In a flash, he pinned Conner to the floor, slamming his face down with a sickening crack.

The rubber chicken's hollow body wrapped around Conner's throat, its absurd squeaks mixing with the sound of panicked screams.

Santa tightened the improvised noose, the chicken's bulbous head pressing into Conner's windpipe.

Conner's arms flailed wildly, his fingers scrabbling for something, anything to fight back. Santa grinned maniacally as he reached for the stapler. With savage glee, he began stapling the chicken to Conner's neck, the sharp clicks of the metal piercing the flesh.

Conner's screams turned to choked gasps as his air was cut off, his vision swimming with dark spots.

The rubber chicken let out one final, pathetic squeak as Santa pulled it tight, his hands slick with Conner's blood,

Santa leaned down, his breath hot against Conner's ear. "Merry Christmas,'" he whispered, his voice dripping with malice.

Conner's body jerked once, twice, and then went still. Santa rose to his feet, his chest heaving as he looked down at his handiwork.

The green room was silent once more.

Justice had been served.

Chapter Sixteen

Onstage, the Thompson Twins flailed through another clunky chorus. The crowd didn't care. The music might as well have been static. They weren't here for them.

They were here for Lee Lauren.

Backstage, Lee stood with his arms crossed, his jaw tightening as the tinny voices grated against his ears. It sounded like cats being strangled. He sighed, already rehearsing the scathing rant he'd unleash on his manager for booking such bargain-bin filler.

But something else gnawed at him. The guards, and how pathetic they looked.

The six young rent-a-cops stood in a loose formation nearby. A few minutes ago, they'd been puffing out their chests, full of swagger at the idea of guarding a star. Now, that bravado had melted. Their eyes weren't on the Twins. They were on the shadow moving closer.

Santa.

The hulking figure stepped out of the gloom, the backstage lights catching on his blood-smeared coat. Upon seeing this, the guards shifted instantly, retreating a step at a time until Lee realised they were positioning themselves behind him, using him as a shield. His brow arched in irritation. Pathetic.

"*Seriously?*" he muttered under his breath. "You know you're supposed to be protecting *me*, right?"

With a roll of his shoulders, Lee stepped forward. He assumed it was just another crazy fan approaching. He'd met his fair share of them. "Uh… who the hell are you?" he snapped, though his voice trembled at the edges.

Santa said nothing at first. He simply tapped the cheap plastic toy cop badge pinned to his chest.

The guards let out visible sighs of relief.

"*Ooooh,*" one said, chuckling nervously. "He's one of *us*."

But the smallest of them, a skinny kid who looked barely out of high school, frowned. His eyes narrowed at the badge, then flicked to the red stains splattered across Santa's coat. "I don't remember seeing you at yesterday's induction. And… what's with the blood?"

"Ah," Santa said smoothly, with the casual air of a man talking about what he had for dinner. "Some kid tried stealing a bag of chips from the self-checkout. Let's just say…" he smiled faintly, "he won't try it again. Not with broken fingers."

The guards chuckled, nodding like it was the most reasonable thing they'd ever heard.

"That'll teach him," one said with a laugh.

Lee pinched the bridge of his nose, muttering, "I'm surrounded by *idiots*."

He turned back to the curtain, parting it just enough to peek at the ocean of teens beyond.

The reaction was instant. The crowd erupted the moment they caught sight of him. A tidal wave of shrieks shook the mall as hundreds of phones shot into the air, their flashes strobing like fireworks. The teens screamed his name in unison, the sound rattling the walls.

Santa stiffened. His eyes flicked to the curtain, his chest heaving as the sound washed over him.

"Those screams…" he whispered, his voice trembling. "They're… for you?"

"*Obviously*," Lee muttered, barely looking at him. He basked in it, soaking up the adoration like sunlight.

Santa's lips parted in awe. He'd heard excitement before, but never like this. Not devotion. Not worship. This was something holy.

"If they're *this* excited, you must have quite the show planned for them," Santa said softly.

Lee barked a laugh. "Show? *Please*. They'll get a smile if I can be bothered. Maybe a wave. Then I take my cheque and go."

Santa blinked, stunned. "But… some of these kids probably travelled many, *many* miles to be here," he pressed, his voice breaking with disbelief. "They came here for *you*. For you to give them something special."

"I couldn't give a shit," Lee replied flatly.

Something twisted inside Santa, hot and poisonous. His fists clenched until his knuckles popped, the sound sharp in the cramped backstage space. His voice dropped to a growl. "That's very… *naughty*. These kids deserve more."

"Piss off, old man."

Santa's chest sank, heavy with sorrow. It was so clear what these children wanted for Christmas. A proper good show. A gift only Lee could give – and that didn't look likely, unfortunately.

Unless…

Santa's mind slipped. As if by some kind of Christmas miracle, he wasn't backstage anymore. He was out there, under the lights. The roar of the crowd hit him like a tidal wave, drowning him in pure, frenzied devotion. His face rippled, smoothed, youth spilling back into his features. His jaw sharpened. Blond hair thickened, gleamed under the stage lights. Until the reflection staring back at him wasn't his own. It was Lee Lauren's.

The red velvet dissolved into a glittering jacket that shimmered with every breath.

"*Lee! Lee! Lee!*" the crowd chanted, the sound shaking his ribs, filling his bones with electricity. Girls screamed until their voices broke. Boys pumped fists, begging for a glance. Phones flashed like fireworks, desperate to capture every moment of him.

He strutted across the stage, arms wide, bathing in their love. In a mirrored prop at the stage's edge, he ran his fingers through silky blond hair that wasn't his. His reflection smirked back at him — Lee's perfect face where Santa's should've been.

97

And then the illusion shattered, splintering like glass. The roar of the crowd evaporated. The glittering lights went dark. All that remained was the reek of dust, stale sweat, and the flat thud of the Thompson Twins' final chorus bleeding through the curtains.

Santa blinked, the brightness draining from his eyes. He leaned toward Lee, his voice low, almost pleading, "*Go on*, kid. *Please*. Give the children a proper show. It'll make their Christmas."

Lee snorted, brushing him off like a stray fly. "I don't give a shit about their Christmas."

"*Well I do!*" Santa roared.

The outburst cracked through the area like a whip, jolting the rent-a-cops and even sending Lee a step back, his smug mask slipping. The guards exchanged uneasy glances, hands hovering near their belts, but none of them dared move closer.

Santa's chest heaved, every breath sharp with fury and something deeper — conviction. Slowly, his lips curled into a smile. Not the jovial grin of a shopping-mall Saint Nick, but something darker. Hungrier. A promise.

"And I'll see to it," he growled, his voice steady now, brimming with grim certainty, "that they get what they want."

Chapter Seventeen

Kieran stood at the back of the massive crowd of Lee Lauren fans, his arms folded, a faint scowl tugging at the corners of his mouth. The director of Merryvale Shopping Mall hadn't wanted to attend this spectacle, but curiosity - and the staggering appearance fee he'd paid - had dragged him here. Everyone seemed so obsessed with the celebrity, he wanted to see what all the fuss was about.

The Thompson Twins were near the end of their performance, assaulting the audience with their rendition of 'You Win Again' by The Bee Gees. Kieran cringed as they ham-fistedly altered the lyrics to "You Twin Again," smugly nodding at each other like they'd reinvented the wheel. The crowd, predictably, ignored them, their energy solely reserved for the arrival of Lee Lauren.

Backstage, a much darker scene was unfolding.

Santa stood in the shadows, his breathing slow and deliberate as he prepared for his transformation. His fingers tightened around the handle of his bloody knife in his pocket. A glint of madness shone in his eyes, a man utterly consumed by his delusion.

One of the rent-a-cops saw the knife first. His face blanched as his gaze flicked to Santa's maniacal grin. *"Ah, shit,"* he muttered under his breath, nudging the guard beside him.

"What?" this second guard asked. Then he saw it too - Santa's unwavering gaze, the bloodied blade, the unsettling calmness radiating from him. His stomach turned as dread clawed its way up his spine.

"Ah, shit," the second guard whispered urgently, nudging the next in line.

The warning passed like a wave through the group, each guard's face paling as they became aware of the impending threat. The logical thing to do for people in their position would have been to stand together, combine their strengths and subdue the lunatic before things escalated. But that was logic. What rose in their chests wasn't reason - it was terror.

As one, they bolted.

Santa didn't flinch as the guards scattered like leaves in the wind, their footsteps echoing in the empty backstage corridors. He expected nothing less from such weaklings. Their cowardice wasn't even worth acknowledging.

Lee Lauren turned just in time to see his supposed security detail fleeing the scene. Confusion twisted his expression. *"The fuck?"* he barked after them, his frustration building.

Then he looked towards Santa.

He froze in place upon seeing Santa's eyes. They burned with a chilling mix of hatred and purpose, the kind of look that promised violence.

Lee Lauren's breath caught in his throat. His gaze dropped to the knife, the reality of the situation crashing down on him like a tidal wave. There was no mistaking Santa's intent. All the terrified celebrity could say at this moment was, "*Ah, fuck.*"

Santa gripped Lee Lauren's perfectly styled hair with one bloodied hand, yanking the celebrity's head toward the glinting blade in the other. The sharp metallic scent of blood mixed with Lee's expensive cologne, the latter fading fast as terror consumed him. He barely managed to choke out a plea before the blade bit into his flesh.

Out front, Kieran remained oblivious to the carnage unfolding backstage. He watched as The Thompson Twins took their final bow. Not a single clap followed. The silence was broken only by Tommy Thompson's awkwardly chipper question: "Before we bring on Lee Lauren, who wants to hear one last song from us?"

The crowd answered with a deafening, unanimous, "*No!*"

Tammy pouted. "*Fine.* Let's bring out Lee Lauren."

With that, the crowd erupted into ear-piercing screams of excitement, a cacophony that made Kieran wince. "I'm too old for this crap," he muttered, glancing at his watch.

A booming dance track exploded from the speakers, its brain-rotting refrain — *"She's got bacon-flavoured titties!"* — pulsing in sync with the strobes and lasers. Foam cannons hissed to life, blasting the crowd with thick, white froth that reeked of something wrong. Not sweet, not synthetic. Acrid. Chemical.

Kieran sniffed the air, his nose wrinkling. *Gasoline?* He thought better of it. No one would be stupid enough.

Then the headliner arrived.

Or rather, something *wearing* the headliner.

The crowd's deafening cheers wavered, faltered, dissolved into uneasy murmurs as Santa skipped into the spotlight. He was dressed — if you could call it that — in the remains of Lee Lauren. The pop star's sequined jacket was ripped wide across Santa's chest, splitting at the seams as if trying to flee his body. The jeans clung desperately to his thighs, refusing to stretch any higher than his blood-slicked knees. Above them, sagging, shit-stained underwear hung on full display, yellow and brown smears illuminated under the strobes. A grotesque parody of youth and glamour.

But it was the head that froze the audience in place.

Santa *wore* Lee's face.

The pop star's once-perfect features were draped over him like a butchered mask, edges curling and peeling, blood dripping in rivulets down Santa's neck. The skin sagged where it didn't align with his own. Lee's lips drooped lopsided, his nose caved where bone had been shattered, one eyelid fluttered uselessly above Santa's own eye. It was both recognisable and hideously wrong — a waxwork effigy left too close to a fire.

The Thompson Twins froze mid-step, their synchronised smiles collapsing into rictus horror. Their routine disintegrated as they stumbled back, eyes wide, as the hulking figure lumbered between them.

Santa, oblivious or in denial, twirled. He strutted. He waved at the audience like a model parading couture, convinced this grotesque ensemble was dazzling them.

Then the first scream ripped through the silence — and the hysteria began.

The crowd erupted, a tidal wave of terror surging for the exits. Teenagers trampled one another, sneakers slamming into ribs and faces as bodies went down. Foam made the floor a deathtrap, slick and unstable. Some fell and didn't rise. Others collapsed mid-sprint, overcome by shock. The shrieks of devotion that had once filled the mall were replaced by shrieks of animal panic, the thunder of bodies slamming into barricades, the crash of glass as shopfronts shattered under the stampede.

At the back, Kieran didn't move. He drew calmly on his cigarette, smoke curling from his nostrils. "Well," he muttered, ember glowing in the dark, "that's the end of the mall. Fun while it lasted."

On stage, Santa's chest heaved. His heart pounded in his ears. No — this wasn't right. They were supposed to cheer. They were supposed to *love* him. He clutched the microphone, his voice booming out warped and frantic through the speakers.

"Wait! Don't run! I've got a great show for you! Songs! Dances!"

The stampede didn't slow.

His hands trembled as he fumbled at his face, peeling the grotesque mask of Lee Lauren away and holding it high like proof. "It's okay! It's *me*! It's *Santa*! Relax! I'm Santa Claus!"

If anything, the panic only intensified.

Down front, the foam sloshed around Kieran's boots. He flicked his cigarette to the ground and went to grind it out — but the instant flame touched froth, the truth hit him.

It was *indeed* gasoline.

Fire roared up his body in an instant, engulfing him in a pillar of flame. He didn't even have time to scream before collapsing, his charred corpse crumpling in on itself.

The blaze spread with terrifying speed. The foam wasn't decoration; it was accelerant. Flames licked across the floor, up the walls, consuming teens as they ran. Hair and clothing ignited. Flesh bubbled and split. The acrid stench of burning bodies filled the air, clinging thick to every breath.

Smoke swallowed the stage, churning black and suffocating. The music blared on, grotesquely cheerful against the backdrop of death.

At the centre of it all stood Santa, frozen.

His borrowed face sagged, melting in the heat. His gloved fists clenched around the microphone. His voice cracked, desperate, shrill:

"No! This isn't how it's supposed to be! C'mon, guys… *I'm Santa*. You're supposed to *love me!* Not *fear* me!"

But there was no love left.

Only fire, panic, and screams.

Chapter Eighteen

Santa staggered through the inferno, each step swallowed by the chaos around him — screams that shredded throats, the crackle of fire devouring foam and flesh, the groan of steel as the mall began to give way.

The stench was unbearable. Burning polyester, charred skin, acrid gasoline smoke — it clawed down his throat and filled his lungs, but he marched on as though immune. His gloved hands shook as he pulled his red coat back over his blistered shoulders, fumbling with the buttons. It didn't feel right to have ever taken it off. That was a mistake. The suit was who he was. But he had done it for the kids.

In his other hand, Lee Lauren's face dangled, a grotesque trophy. The heat had already begun to warp it, the skin bubbling and sagging, the lips drooping open in a silent, mocking O. It no longer resembled the idol the teens had once screamed for — only a mask melting into sludge.

As Santa stumbled forward, the fleeing crowd instinctively split around him, their shrieks rising as if he carried the fire itself.

Wide eyes followed his hulking frame, their terror etched so clearly it should have shattered him. But he fought to twist their horror into something else, something he could bear.

In his mind, a voice broke through the chaos — high-pitched, trembling but worshipful. *"Great show, Santa! You almost had me convinced you were the real Lee Lauren!"*

His chest swelled at the phantom praise. "You're welcome," he whispered to himself, lips cracking into a smile as soot smeared across his teeth.

"They love me," he muttered, almost chanting it now. "They really love me."

But the fantasy splintered with every glance at their faces. They weren't dazzled. They were petrified. Their screams weren't chants. They were pleas. His delusion tried to stitch the images together — the mall transforming into a magical stage one moment, only to snap back into hellfire the next. Glittering spotlights blurred into burning rafters, adoring fans into stampeding cattle, applause into the agonised wails of children.

Santa swayed on his feet, teetering between the dream and the nightmare, unable to tell which was real anymore.

Tears streamed down his soot-covered cheeks as he reached the mall's main exit. The glass doors had been shattered in the panic, and he stepped over the shards, leaving bloody footprints in his wake. Outside, the cold night air hit his blistered skin, a stark contrast to the inferno he left behind.

Red and blue lights painted the parking lot, and sirens wailed in the distance. Police cars screeched to a halt in front of him, their doors flying open as officers poured out, guns drawn.

Santa stood still, swaying slightly, his bloodstained hands hanging at his sides. The officers hurriedly approached, shouting commands he barely registered.

"They *love* me too," he thought with a fragile smile. He closed his eyes, imagining the officers running to hug him, congratulating him on a performance that had touched their hearts.

The harsh grip of handcuffs shattered the illusion.

The metal bit into his wrists, forcing him to the ground. His knees hit the pavement hard, jolting him back to reality. He looked up at the officers, his face a mixture of confusion and disappointment. "Did I do something wrong? They still love me... right?"

The questions were ignored.

One officer guided him into the back of a squad car. Santa slumped into the seat, the weight of the cuffs pulling his arms awkwardly behind him.

As the car sped away, another one of the officers glanced at him through the rearview mirror. "That's quite the mess you left back there," he said, his tone dry.

Santa sighed, his voice heavy with regret. "I completely forgot about the gasoline in the foam. They definitely would have loved me if it weren't for the gasoline... right?"

The officer raised an eyebrow, glancing at the blood-streaked, delirious man. "Suuure they would have," he muttered sarcastically. "Crazy bastard."

Then, recognition flickered across the cop's face. His eyes narrowed as he studied Santa in the mirror. "Wait a sec. You're the Merryvale Santa! The guy from that viral video!"

Santa gave a weak nod. "Yeah. That's me."

The officer let out a low chuckle. "Well, ain't this something? I'm taking Santa to jail on Christmas Eve. Guess people won't be opening any of your gifts tomorrow."

A faint smirk crossed Santa's lips. He turned his gaze to the window, watching the flashing lights blur against the night. "That's not *quite* true," he murmured.

***

On the afternoon of Christmas Day, the atmosphere was thick with tension in one particular household - the home of the teenage boy who had antagonised Santa and filmed the aftermath, starting this whole fiasco.

The boy's mother sat at the kitchen table, wringing her hands nervously.

"We should wait for him," she said softly, glancing at her husband.

The man's hand shot out, slapping her hard across the face. "Don't you ever tell me what to do, woman," he growled.

109

She cowered, holding her cheek, as he loomed over her.

"If that boy doesn't want to be with his family on Christmas Day, that's his choice," the man spat. "I'm not putting the day on hold for his selfishness."

In the living room, a large, elaborately wrapped box had been sitting untouched for days. It was addressed to the father, and he'd been itching to open it since it arrived. Unable to wait any longer, he strode over to it, his anger momentarily replaced with childlike anticipation.

He tore through the wrapping paper and opened the box, eager to see what lay inside.

The moment his eyes fell on the contents, he froze. His face twisted into an expression of pure, unfiltered terror.

Inside the box was the lifeless, contorted body of his son. Blood pooled at the bottom, staining the festive wrapping paper.

The man stumbled backwards, his legs giving out beneath him as he collapsed to the floor. "No," he whispered, shaking his head. "No, no, no!"

He began to scream, the sound raw and guttural, as tears streamed down his face. The mother rushed into the room, her own scream joining his when she saw what was inside.

***

At that very moment, miles away, Santa sat alone in his cell, staring at the cold concrete walls. The faint sound of holiday music drifted in from the guards' break room, a cheery juxtaposition to the bleakness around him.

He closed his eyes, picturing the scene unfolding in the boy's house. In his mind, the father was smiling as he opened the box. "Finally, we're rid of that no-good brat," he imagined the man saying. "It's a Christmas miracle. Thank you, Santa! I love you."

A small, satisfied smile tugged at Santa's lips.

"*I love you too*," he whispered to the empty cell.

The End.

Acknowledgements

To my fellow lovers of horror: *thank you*.

Thank you for reading my books with open minds, strong stomachs, and zero judgment. You've embraced the dark corners of my imagination without flinching, and that means more to me than you know.

To those of you who have read every gory detail, indulged in the absurdity, and still wanted more - you're my kind of people.

To the brave souls who have recommended my stories to friends and family, fully knowing they might question your sanity - I salute you.

Finally, to horror itself: you twisted, wonderful genre. You've been a playground, a therapist, and an unflinching mirror. Without you, there'd be no catharsis, no thrill, and certainly no books like this.

Q&A

What inspired you to write this book?

A deep love of horror, a mild obsession with holiday chaos, and a nagging question: What if the world's most jolly saint snapped? Combine that with some caffeine-fuelled brainstorming, and this story practically wrote itself.

Is Santa based on anyone you know?

Well... yeah. *Santa*!

Do you actually enjoy Christmas?

Yes and no. Christmas is a bit of a double-edged sword - it can be the most magical time of year or the most challenging, depending on where you are in life. I've had some really tough Christmases in the past, where the season only amplified how difficult things were. But right now, I'm in a good place, and I have a 6-year-old who's completely enchanted by the festive magic. Seeing it all through his eyes makes it feel special in a way I've never experienced before. This year, I'm genuinely so excited for it.

Are the Thompson Twins based on real people?

Sort of - they're loosely based on myself, or at least the version of me when I was first starting out as a holiday entertainer many *MANY* years ago. Back then, I thought I had to be this over-the-top ball of energy, high-fiving everyone and acting like I was running on pure caffeine. It was exhausting. Over time, I learned to tone it down and just be myself. The Thompson Twins are like a caricature of that overenthusiastic phase of my life - dialled up to 11.

Will there be a Really Naughty List sequel?

Never say never. If there's one thing horror has taught us, it's that villains have a knack for coming back when you least expect it. Plus, I had a lot of fun writing this character and feel there's more to explore with him.

Any advice for aspiring horror writers?

Don't hold back. Write what scares you, what excites you, and what makes other people say, "Are you okay?" The best horror comes from the parts of your imagination you're almost too afraid to explore.

Are you okay?

Physically or mentally?

Physically.

...Meh.

And mentally?

...Meh.

What's your favourite horror movie or book?

That's such a tough question! I have a soft spot for The Blair Witch Project. I saw it way back before I even had the internet at home (yes, I'm definitely dating myself here). I went in completely blind, with no idea it was fictional, so for the longest time, I genuinely thought it was real. That level of immersion and fear stuck with me - there's just something timeless about how it plays with your imagination.

A few years back, I re-watched the film in an actual woods. There's a video of this on my YouTube Channel (Another Bloody Youtuber) if you're interested.

Final thoughts?

Again, thank you so much for reading, for diving headfirst into this madness, and for loving horror as much as I do. If you enjoyed this, please tell your friends. If you didn't... well, maybe keep that to yourself. Sorry, couldn't resist recycling that old holiday entertainer joke one last time!

The Very Naughty List (Part Two)

I'm thrilled to share that **The Very Naughty List: Part Two** is finally here!

If you thought Part 1 was wild... you haven't seen *anything* yet. This sequel let me push my imagination even further, and I can't wait for you to dive in.

The story picks up almost one year after the Merryvale Massacre. Santa has become more than a monster — he's an icon. Across the globe, people have started writing him letters, not with wish lists, but with names. Bosses, abusers, liars, killers — the people they want gone. What they *really* want for Christmas is for Santa to kill on their behalf.

And Santa, being Santa, would love nothing more than to grant those wishes. The only problem? He's trapped in prison. But maybe — just maybe — with a little Christmas magic, he'll find a way...

Here's a sneak peek at **Part Two**. I hope you enjoy it as much as I loved writing it.

Being a senior journalist for one of the world's largest media conglomerates, Paul Elliot was no stranger to hysteria. He'd elbowed his way through rabid fans to get to A-listers, politicians, and even disgraced royals. But never - not once - had he seen crowds like this gathered for a serial killer.

The car slowed to a crawl as it pushed through the sea of screaming fans outside the prison gates. Posters and signs waved like desperate prayers in a twisted nativity parade: 'Justice for Santa', 'We Love You Santa', and one scrawled in glitter glue that read, 'Please Let Me Suck Your Baubles'.

Paul chuckled. "*Jesus*," he muttered under his breath. "*Merry bloody Christmas.*"

They were lined up in droves behind barricades, dressed in red, white, and faux fur, some with fake beards, some crying, some livestreaming.

From his seat, Paul could see the outer gates of the prison beginning to part. A squad of armed guards stood between him and the entrance, keeping the crowd at bay.

Paul was a man with dwarfism, barely four feet tall, but there was nothing small about him - certainly not where it counted. His presence filled a room long before his footsteps did. Where others used height to command attention, Paul used language. Words were his height, his reach, his weapon.

His columns had made careers, crushed reputations, and flipped public sentiment like a coin. He knew too well the power of the pen - not as a metaphor, but as a fact. To Paul, the pen wasn't mightier than the sword. It was the sword. And he'd drawn it more times than he could count.

Now, as the gates of the prison slid open and the crowd's roar began to fade behind him, Paul straightened the cuffs of his coat and took a steadying breath. Somewhere beyond those grey concrete walls and clusters of security cameras was his next great story.

Maybe even his *greatest yet*.

Before long, Paul was seated across from the warden in his office. The room was deliberately bare - by necessity, not style. Over the years, plenty of inmates had been brought in here, and anything not nailed down could be turned into a weapon.

The man behind the desk was Mr. Bain, a hardened relic of the prison system. His face told the story: deep, weathered scars carved across his cheeks and temple - souvenirs from a career spent in the thick of it. Bain wasn't the kind of man who stayed behind glass when things went sideways. He threw himself into the chaos - breaking up brawls, dragging inmates apart, and more than once taking a blow meant for someone else. Some battles he won. Others, not so much. But he never backed down.

Paul, holding a modest gift hamper in his lap, eyed the man carefully. He recognised a bribe when he saw one.

"It's a few of your favourite things," Bain said with uncharacteristic cheer, gesturing toward the basket like a proud uncle. "Just to say thanks... for coming all this way."

Paul started to unpack the items. First came a bottle of centuries-old whisky - his favourite brand, aged longer than most of the inmates in this place. Then, a bundle of rare Cuban cigars, meticulously wrapped. There was also a delicate box of chocolates from a tiny artisan shop in the remote north of Denmark. He hadn't tasted them since a childhood trip he once called the happiest week of his life - in print, no less.

Paul raised an eyebrow. "You've done your homework."

But just as he was about to set the basket aside, something moved beneath the shredded packaging. A sudden shift - soft, warm, alive. He reached in cautiously and pulled out a tiny ginger kitten, blinking up at him with wide blue eyes and a soft mewl.

"…What's... *this*?" Paul asked, bewildered.

The warden's face twisted in confusion, then embarrassment. "I—I spoke to someone you know," he stammered, "and they said you loved nothing more than puss—" He froze mid-word. A realisation dawned. "*Ah*. Okay. I see where this went wrong."

Without further comment, Bain opened a desk drawer, gently placed the kitten inside, and slid it shut.

Paul cleared his throat. "The gifts are generous, Warden Bain. But *unnecessary*. If you'd dug a little deeper, you'd know - I don't take bribes. Now… why don't we get down to business?"

"*Of course*," Bain replied, the cheer in his voice fading. He rose from his chair, clasped his hands behind his back, and wandered toward the window. The blinds were tilted just enough for him to peer across the outer yard, where the crowd outside the prison gates continued to grow - faces pressed to the fencing, voices carrying faintly through the glass.

"A few dozen fans showed up yesterday," he said. "By this morning, it was *hundreds*. And if the internet's anything to go by, this is just the beginning. We're bracing for a flood. A full-blown *tsunami*."

He nodded toward the corner of the room, where an oversized mail sack sagged under its own weight.

"Those came in this morning. Actual letters... *to Santa*. From *fully grown adults*. And get this... they're not asking Santa for train sets or cuddly toys. They're asking him to *kill people*. That's their wish. For him to *murder* on their behalf."

Paul leaned in toward the mail. "May I take a peek?"

Bain nudged the sack with his foot, and Paul reached in, pulling a handful of envelopes free. Most were covered in glitter, stickers, or crayon drawings. One was scrawled in elegant cursive and sealed with wax. As he flipped through them, he discreetly slipped one into his coat pocket.

Bain didn't seem to notice. He was back at the window, his jaw clenched.

"Some of my staff are already pulling out of next week's Christmas Eve parade," Bain said, his voice tight. "They're scared the public's going to turn on them. We've had a few emails. Threats. Demands to release Santa, or they'll kill us."

He exhaled heavily, the tension visibly dragging at his posture.

"I think it's nonsense, of course - empty threats from the usual breed of keyboard-warrior lunatics. But still, my team's rattled,

120

and I'd like to put their minds at ease. It only took one article to spark this blaze. Maybe another can put it out - if it's written by the right person. The best. *You.*"

Paul gave a thoughtful nod, his eyes narrowing as he reached for his notepad.

"I'll certainly see what I can do, Mr. Bain," Paul said evenly, flicking his pen open with a quiet click. "Let's start simple. In your own words - why do *you* think the public's so angry?"

Bain scoffed under his breath. "It's that *goddamn article,*" he muttered. "Some gutter rag ran a piece turning Clarkson into a folk hero. Called him a saviour in a red suit. Claimed everyone he killed *deserved* it."

He moved to a filing cabinet, opened it absently, then shut it again without taking anything out - just something to do with his hands.

"Lee Lauren? Supposedly used his fame to rape underage fans - so now Clarkson's a protector of children. Connor, the mall's head of security? Said to have shattered teenage bones on the job. Brutal 'discipline,' he called it. Complaints were rarely taken seriously. Management swept them under the rug."

Bain turned back to Paul, his voice sharper now.

"Which leads me to Kieran Poole - the Mall owner. They say he strangled small businesses with rent hikes. Families ruined. People on the street. That one stuck hard with folks. Hit a nerve."

He paused, as if trying to keep himself from laughing.

121

"Then it got ridiculous. Lord Steeler? He was apparently rude to waiters. Liz Lang? She was a *vegan*. That's all it took for the public to agree that they, too, deserved to die. Clarkson became a one-man moral compass."

Paul looked up from his notepad, his eyes cool and unreadable. "And do *you* think they deserved to die?"

Bain shot him a glare sharp enough to cut glass. "Is that a serious question?"

Paul didn't flinch. "It is. I'm just trying to get the full picture."

The warden exhaled hard through his nose and turned back toward the window, his silhouette etched against the grey. "Look… if we started killing everyone who's ever done anything shitty, there wouldn't be anyone left. Everyone's got skeletons - some just buried deeper than others. You dig hard enough, you can paint anyone as the villain."

Paul studied him carefully, catching the weight in his voice - the cracks forming beneath the stoic surface. Then, from somewhere beyond the walls, a shrill voice pierced the air.

"Release him or die!"

It echoed, distant but clear, like a prophecy hurled over the wind.

Paul didn't look away. "If you could wave a magic Panto wand," he said evenly, "what would you want me to write in this article of mine?"

Bain hesitated, his jaw tense. Then: "That Sam Clarkson is not a saviour. He's not - God help me for even needing to say this - not the real Santa Claus. These people didn't die for some noble reason. They died because they fired him. And as they should have. Because the man is unwell. Dangerous. Delusional. That's the story. That's *the truth*."

Paul nodded. "I'll keep that in mind. But before I start writing... I need to speak to him."

"*Santa?*" Bain asked, then immediately winced. "Sorry - *Clarkson? Why?*"

"Because if you want this story told right," Paul said, closing his notebook, "Like I said... I need the full picture."

Bain instinctively shook his head. "That's... not standard procedure."

"But you know as well as I do - this isn't a standard case." Paul leaned forward, his tone quiet but firm. "If you want this article... I need to speak to him. *Alone.* No guards. No cameras. No wires. He needs my trust, and I need *yours*."

The warden hesitated, his lips drawn tight in a line. Then, finally, he muttered: "...*Fine.*"

The Devil's Replacement (Chapter One)

Another book I've written similar to this one is titled, The Devil's Replacement.

"Wonderfully dark horror comedy!" - Sharron Joy Reads

"Clever, Entertaining and Thought-Provoking." - Jai Hui

"So entertaining, I could not put it down!" - Holly Schultz

"Finally! A twist I didn't expect." - Aaron

The Devil is ready to retire from ruling Hell.

Before settling down with his sex crazed girlfriend, he must first seek a worthy replacement.

Through a series of gripping and connected short horror stories, we meet a variety of candidates potentially ready to take the reins.

From the twisted ringmaster of a circus that contains a dark secret, to an unstable superhuman saviour who begins to question whether society deserves to be punished rather than protected, each individual has their own unique, thrilling, twisted and often hilarious story to tell.

Only one of them will ultimately get the job. **Place your bets.**

Unsure if this story is for you? Here's the first chapter to help you decide!

"Welcome to Hell!"

"Welcome to Hell. My name is Hitler and I'll be your guide," said the former German Führer in a joyful and welcoming tone.

He stood, confident; front and centre on the upper deck of a classic red tour bus whilst two-dozen passengers looked on towards him, bemusement written across their faces.

A myriad of brightly lit structures whizzed past them with the bus reaching a speed far greater than any of these passengers would have ever experienced before now. It was as if they were hurtling through a Vegas strip that seemed to have no end. Further similarities included the abundance of sinners.

Like most new hordes of wrongdoers, their perplexed reactions were predictable. Stereotypical even, given that most newcomers struggled to process that they had just died, let alone been condemned to an abyss of pain and suffering.

It would be fair to assume though, a majority of these bewildered gawps would be as a consequence of Hitler modelling a new look he'd been contemplating for a while. His military attire remained, like he'd stepped straight out from the history books. However, the neatly squared moustache he was infamous for (amongst other things) had been grown out, creating long curls at each end - much like a Victorian, melodramatic villain.

It didn't take long for one of the passengers to query this obvious transformation. Barry Jeffrey raised his hand. Back on Earth, this obese monstrosity was a chief executive officer for a third world children's charity. The underworld was rarely home to philanthropists, which, on paper, he appeared to be. In reality, he'd often gorge himself with extravagant meals, using money stolen from the charity's funds that were actually meant for life saving solutions for starving kids. The irony.

Upon seeing the thief's hand raised, Hitler asked, "Yes, Barry. How can I help?"

"I have a question."

"I've no doubt that you do. You're in Hell and face to face with a World War legend. I expect you have *many* questions. Your mind must be frickin' blown right now! Luckily, we have a few minutes before reaching our first destination, so I'm happy to answer anything from anyone within that short amount of time. Shoot."

"We're in Hell? So... we're dead?"

"We prefer the term 'life challenged'. But, yes."

"And... you're Hitler?" Barry continued suspiciously. "Like, *the* Hitler?"

"Do you know of many others?" the guide replied, playfully. "Yes, I am he. Your Dark Lord found that people generally tend to freak out less when they're presented with a familiar face once they reach Hell."

"If a familiar face is so important... why lose the Charlie Chaplin moustache?"

The former Führer began to look rather self-conscious, scratching away at the facial hair as if he were trying to conceal it. "Any questions from anyone else?" he snapped, ignoring the initial query.

Another hand went up. This time it was that of Louise Fryer. This dark soul had been destined for Hell ever since playing God at the hospital she'd worked at for numerous years. During that time, many lives had perished as a result of the nurse switching medication and adjusting significant notes left by doctors. This was all simply to overcome her boredom.

"Yes, what's your question, Louise?" Hitler asked.

"Have you styled your moustache any other ways throughout the years?"

"Seriously?" the guide shouted furiously. "David Beckham used to have a different hairstyle once every frickin' week. Apparently, I can't even have a different style once every frickin' century. Any other questions?"

Ten other hands raised.

Frustrated, Hitler continued, "Any questions that are not, in any way, related to my facial hair?"

All but one hand lowered. Paul Stevens' crime was arguably the most sickening compared to those sat around him, at least in the eyes of the Second World War leader. This offender was a music producer who had found himself in this situation due to his crimes against music. It was he who had discovered a young, obnoxious 'singer' and unleashed the brat on the world, resulting in the torture of billions of innocent ears.

"Yes... dickhead over there. What's your question?" Hitler asked sharply, still pissed off that it had taken weeks for him to get the song 'Baby, oooooh, baby' out of his head.

Paul sheepishly queried, "What happens to us once we get off this bus?"

Right on cue, the vehicle began to slow its speed significantly. "You're about to find out, Paul," Hitler said, sinisterly, whilst twirling the ends of his moustache.

The bus came to a complete halt beside a large concert hall. The doors to the vehicle and that of the music venue opened in unison. With a mere few metres in length between the two, it couldn't have been clearer to the music producer the path he was encouraged to take, and so, he apprehensively walked towards his fate.

Inside the grand venue was a manifestation of the vile child star he had discovered, waiting to sing his 'Baby, oooooh, baby' hit. Paul, the one and only audience member, amidst thousands of empty seats, was now destined to be trapped for an eternity, listening to the rascal performing that one song, over and over and over again.

This particular punishment was, of course, unique to the individual - as was the practice with all those who had been summoned to Hell. Each sentence was tailored to fit poetically with each heinous crime committed.

For example, Barry Jeffrey would soon be tied to a chair, his wrists and ankles bound tightly with ropes. He'd then have a tube forced down his throat by a malnourished young boy, who would pump a never ending supply of blended food into the CEO's body. This would muffle all cries for help.

"No, thank you... I don't want any," the boy would say, mockingly. "You need this more than I do. Honestly, I'm used to not eating – so, you go ahead and enjoy."

Before long, Barry would have involuntarily gorged himself to death. At that point, he'd reset to his former ravenous state, physically ready for a fresh array of dishes whilst mentally knowing the excruciating pain that lay ahead.

Furthermore, Louise Fryer's punishment would see her become a human version of the popular children's game, Operation. Each one of her previous victims would take great pleasure in using tweezers to remove body parts without touching the edge of the cavity. For theatrical effect, the nurse's nose would even glow red whenever they would fail. Yes, just like in the game.

After dropping off the final passenger, Hitler headed home - exhausted from such a long shift. All he wanted to do was watch people suffering on the television whilst crashed out on the couch. The problem was, he knew that his housemate/boss, Satan, would likely have other plans for him.

The Devil and he became acquainted many decades before. Satan quickly saw the benefits of having a natural leader by his side, officially delegating him the role of assistant manager. It started off with a little account filing here and then some project management there - but before long, the ruler of Hell was expecting more and more from the former Führer. By masterfully choosing to move Hitler into his own home, the Devil was able to take his exhausting commands to the next level - such as demanding that the house be spotless at all times, food be served in a timely manner and... well, absolutely any other tasks delegated to his 'Devil Bitch' - a name gifted to Hitler from Satan.

Why would someone tolerate such psychological and often physical torment? Well, for starters, upset the Devil once and you'll never intentionally do so again. Some of the most recent punishments included Hitler bathing in waters with unimaginable temperatures, so high that the skin would peel away like a piece of fruit. There was also the time that he was sentenced to driving through Britain's M25 motorway during rush-hour at the peak of road maintenance - neither of which the World War 2 leader wanted to experience ever again. It was unbearable.

Another notable reason that stood out as a justification for putting up with the abuse, was the promise that one day, should Satan ever wish to retire, the position of ruler would be given to his, 'Devil Bitch'.

With each passing decade, however, Hitler became less convinced of this promise ever transpiring but clung onto the little hope he had left.

Now, you may be wondering what kind of home the likes of Satan and Hitler would choose to reside in? Pop culture references would likely have you believe that the Devil lived in some fiery cave, or perhaps perched upon a throne, made from the skulls once belonging to the damned, on constant watch of the ever-growing number of sinners.

Reality couldn't have been further from these assumptions. They actually inhabited a rather lovely, modest, two-bedroom cottage. The only flames being those coming from their antique marble fireplace, with the one and only item linked in any way to death being their genuine leather couch.

Many would also assume that Satan's physical appearance was that of a fanged, horned demon and whilst this would sometimes be the case, nobody knew exactly what the Devil looked like in his original, true form - not even his roomie of many years. The Dark Lord would simply masquerade in whatever form he chose at the time. It would often be the classic demon figure taking shape one day, but it could be the uncanny resemblance of a world leader the next. Heck, he once spent an entire week streaking naked in the form of Hitler with a micro-penis because he thought it'd be hilarious if everyone thought Hitler had a... well, micro-penis. Most onlookers commented on how this explained his outbursts of rage.

Have you ever read articles of once loved and seemingly angelic celebrities acting despicably out of character? Maybe, just maybe, you were actually bearing witness to the Devil himself. For example, a former Pope had always sworn blind that he had no involvement in ordering a dozen strippers to the Vatican Palace despite the video evidence of him 'making it rain' Euros over the perfectly rounded ass of a lovely lady that went by the name Cinnamon. You'd be right in guessing this was, of course, Satan up to his usual shenanigans.

In recent times, the Devil had mostly been taking the form of a frail old man. This mould of a rather decrepit elderly being was a genuine reflection of how he had been feeling of late. In his defence, ruling the underworld over many millennia would take its toll on anyone.

Upon arriving home, Satan appeared even frailer than he had looked just that morning. Hitler was quick to notice this rapid deterioration in health. Before the Devil had even stepped both feet through the front door, his housemate was rushing to his aid. "You poor thing," he said softly. "You look so tired." Externally, anyone would be convinced that these words were spoken sympathetically. In reality, Hitler was jumping for joy at what lay before him.

"I am absolutely shattered," Satan confirmed before crashing onto the couch with no intention of budging for the remainder of the night.

Hitler was quick to join him and analyse the situation further. "I thought you were heading to a restaurant with one of your girlfriends this evening?"

"I cancelled on Nats. I've just not got the energy right now to keep up with her sexual demands."

"Well, in that case, you can have my dinner, which will be ready in just a jiffy. Until then, maybe you'd like a massage?"

Satan would never say out loud that this was acceptable, but the lowering of his shoulders and general body language indicated that it was okay to proceed. With his hands gripped firmly upon the Devil, this manipulative man continued, "I'm worried. Look at you. Maybe it's finally time you give this all up."

"*Stop*," Satan demanded furiously.

Hitler abruptly put an end to the awkward touching.

"Not the massage," the Devil confirmed, much more tranquil. "This conversation needs to stop. I'm not going to keep having the same discussion over and over again. I'm simply not going to retire. Without ruling Hell, I have nothing."

"You have the knowledge of knowing that for the longest time... you owned it," Hitler said cautiously, trying not to anger his lord too much. "You've caused so much pain and suffering but have never had the free time to actually admire your work."

Satan looked deep in thought before unexpectedly admitting, "Perhaps you're right. I don't think I have it in me to do this much longer. If I were to stand down, though... metaphorically speaking, how would you envision Hell functioning without me?"

Hitler became flustered. This was the furthest the conversation had ever progressed. "Okay," he panicked. "For starters, during my first week of ruling Hell-"

"*Your* first week?"

"Well... *yes*?" Hitler said, confused. "You've always said that if you were to stand down, I would take your place."

133

"I said you *could* take my place. There's a big difference, Devil Bitch."

Hitler looked disheartened. Since day one, he'd never questioned one single request from his master. He did it all. You'll likely not know what it's like taking out the household waste, whilst pocket-sized, feral beasts gnaw away at you in a desperate attempt to get to the contents of those bags. Hitler does. It happened to him every single night to display just one of the numerous examples of his loyalty.

Satan continued, "I've no doubt that you're more than qualified for the job. I merely want to be certain that other potential candidates out there are not just that little bit more suited. I'll interview them, as is the traditional way of doing these things and at the end of the process, if I feel neither is right for the position, the job is yours."

"Do you have candidates in mind?"

"I do. Just four."

Hitler sighed, "Okay, fine - who's the first interviewee?"

"I'll tell you all about her whilst you're giving me my sponge bath."

Printed in Dunstable, United Kingdom